Perhaps it was because he was speaking with such a show of open frankness, that, for a fleeting instant, the novice-master's blocking was incomplete. He spoke approvingly of Raamo's skill, but even as he spoke, Raamo pensed, behind the smiling words, a deep distrust and anxiety.

Until that instant Raamo had made no firm decision concerning Neric and his strange revelations. He had tried to convince himself that Neric had been wrong—and at times he had almost succeeded. He had decided only one thing firmly, and that was that he would do nothing until Neric returned and they had spoken further. But now suddenly, listening to the smiling words of D'ol Regle, and pensing beneath them a coldness that spoke of fear or worse, Raamo found himself saying quickly, "But I have but little skill, D'ol Regle. And what I have had seems to be fading. I am no longer able to pense anything except that which is purposefully sent."

He spoke hastily, lowering his eyes before the surprised stares of not only D'ol Regle, but Genaa, also.

"Indeed?" D'ol Regle questioned. "I had heard that you were able—that your skill was greater?" He paused thoughtfully, and Raamo felt he detected a measure of relief behind the outward show of disappointment. But if D'ol Regle's response to Raamo's lie was devious, Genaa's was frank enough. Although she had no skill at pensing, Raamo found her sending was quite clear and distinct.

"You're lying, Raamo," he pensed. "Why are you lying?"

ZILPHA KEATLEY SNYDER, a three-time Newbery Honor Book–winning author, is also the author of the other books in the Green-sky trilogy—*And All Between* and *Until the Celebration*. She lives in Marin County, California.

Below the Root

Zilpha Keatley Snyder

Published by
Dell Publishing
a division of
Bantam Doubleday Dell Publishing Group, Inc.
666 Fifth Avenue
New York, New York 10103

The trademark Laurel-Leaf Library® is registered in the U.S. Patent and Trademark Office.

The trademark Dell® is registered in the U.S. Patent and Trademark Office.

ISBN: 0-440-21266-9

RL: 7.8

Reprinted by arrangement with the author

Printed in the United States of America

August 1992

10 9 8 7 6 5 4 3 2 1

OPM

To the Kindar

CHAPTER ONE

Seeking a place to be alone, to think and reason and attend to the strange pounding of his heart, Raamo climbed high, until he could almost touch the fronds of the rooftrees. There, among small thin branches, he quickly wove himself a loosely constructed nid and collapsed into it. Already somewhat soothed by the gentle swaying of the high branches, he set out to calm himself further with song, as he had been taught to do since infancy. Choosing the oldest and simplest songs he knew, he began with the slow rhythmic Forest Chant— the first song he could remember learning in his first year at the Garden of Song and Story.

> Forest is and was and will be,
> Root and roof and all between.
> Pan-fruit feed me, nid-bough hold me,
> Peace and Joy be ever green.
>
> Forest is and was and will be,
> Grundtree, rooftree, Sacred Bloom.
> Far and deep our cares are buried,
> By the Wissenroot entombed.

> Forest is and was and will be,
> Where the flight was brought to rest.
> Where the Kindar danced creation,
> By the Ol-zhaan, Spirit blessed.

The song soothed, as always, but not enough. Raamo's heart still raced, and his mind, released from the quiet monotony of the rhythm, leaped back into fevered activity.

Could it be true? Could something so unthinkable really have happened? Could he, Raamo D'ok, who had never been an honor student at the Garden, and who had often received less than perfect marks in Peace and Joy, really have been chosen to join the Ol-zhaan in the temple? It seemed impossible. And yet the Ol-zhaan would not have chosen him mistakenly. In their great wisdom, they must have had good reason. But what could their reasons have been? Racking his mind, Raamo thought back over the years of his life, trying to find clues that might explain the shattering surprise that had, in one brief hour, changed the entire pattern of his existence.

If there had been clues along the way, he had missed them. He had never thought of himself as exceptional. He had been only Raamo D'ok, first-born child of respected but quite ordinary parents—his mother an embroiderer of fine print and his father a harvester of fruit and pan in the Orbora orchards. They were gentle kindly people but undistinguished, with no special skill in learning or Spirit-force.

And Raamo had thought of himself as much the same, or even less praiseworthy. Only an ordinary student at the Garden, he had been given to moodiness and curiosity rather than peacefulness and good memory. Nor was there anything about his appearance that might have given warning. He was, like most Kindar, small boned and slender. As for his face, he seldom made use of a gazing bowl, but he had been told his features were pleasing. However, no one had described them as noble or awe-inspiring. There had really been nothing at all to set him apart, except perhaps for a slightly unusual, if rather unreliable, gift of Spirit-force.

Although he had passed his thirteenth birthday, he still retained some of the Spirit-skills common in young children but usually long outgrown by members of his age group. Yet such children's gifts as pensing, teleporting and grunspreking were surely unrelated to the great all-embracing Spirit-powers of the Ol-zhaan. Still, looking back over his lifetime, Raamo could think of no other possible explanation of any kind.

As far as he could recall, his First Counseling had been entirely unexceptional. He had gone, as did all Kindar children, at the age of three years, to be examined by the Ol-zhaan at the temple. Along with all the infants who had just completed their first year at the Garden, he had been tested and questioned and then sent home.

But today, at his Second Counseling, he had realized almost immediately that something unusual was taking place. From speaking to others who had already attended their Second Counseling, he had expected to stand briefly before a panel of Ol-zhaan who would first congratulate him on having reached the age of full participation in Kindar society. Then records would be consulted, and he would be told what profession had been given him and the day on which his apprenticeship would begin. Unless, of course, and he had thought it highly unlikely, he was chosen for further study at the Academy to prepare for a profession of high honor such as teacher, artist, grund-leader or musician. Should he be so fortunate, he would also be presented with a beautifully embroidered seal of the Academy of Orbora, which he would henceforth wear on the chest of his shuba. But none of these things had happened.

Instead, he had been put aside in a small chamber and left alone for what had seemed to be many hours. Then the Ol-zhaan had come. One alone at first, a woman of great age and beauty, who asked him many questions and stared at him so intently that, on her departure, he was left feeling drained and exhausted. After her, two others, men this time, questioned him more briefly, and they, too, went away. For a long time, Raamo again sat all by himself in the small chamber.

When the Ol-zhaan returned, the two men and the ancient woman, Raamo sprang to his feet and stood waiting, his head bowed respectfully, although he could not resist glancing up at them. He had not often been so near Ol-zhaan and he found them beautiful and awful, their faces noble and full of dignity, their white shubas, decorated with seals of gold and green, almost dazzling in their splendor.

And then they had told him. Told him, Raamo D'ok, that he was to be a Chosen, and that the announcement of his choosing would be made to all the inhabitants of Green-sky at the next assembly.

The thought of that announcement and what would follow filled Raamo with awe and wonder and a troubling disquiet. Reaching up to brush a trailing tendril of Wis-senvine away from his eyes, Raamo noticed that his fingers were still quivering like the fronds of a rooftree in a high wind. Holding out both hands, he studied the quivering with interest. Was he ill, or was this shaking related to the quickened beat of his heart? He had seen such quivering in the ailing or the very old. Suddenly Raamo found himself wishing that he had a handful of Wissenberries. He did not use them often, since the sensation they produced was not to his liking, but at this moment the soothing drowsy effect of the Berry might seem a blessing. Lifting his head, Raamo looked around him without any real hope of finding Wissenberries; the Vine rarely produced blossoms or fruit at such high altitudes. Just as he expected, the Vine that curtained his hideaway, and of which he had woven his makeshift resting place, was barren, producing nothing but small sun-blighted leaves and the thinnest of tendrils.

Impatiently Raamo climbed out of his hammock and prepared to descend. He was going to look for Wissenberries—or perhaps not. Perhaps he was just going to look for—someone to speak to. Poised on the narrow branch, he glanced down, picking out the best glide path, one that would take him down to the midheights with a minimum of stops. A few steps out on an adjoining branch put him in position to take advantage of a long corridor relatively free of branches or curtains of Vine. With a few skillful turns, he would be able to glide almost to his nid-place without stopping or climbing. He stood on the narrow grundbranch, looking down hundreds of feet, through vast open spaces softly lit by filtering rays of greenish light, bordered and intersected by enormous branches, festooned with curtains of graceful Wissenvine. Shaking out the wing-panels of his shuba, the long silken robe worn by all except the youngest infants, he launched himself downward into space.

He drifted slowly, enjoying the freedom of the glide, the downward tug of gravity, the occasional lift of rising currents of air, and feeling the tug of his shuba cuffs on wrists and ankles as he skillfully shifted the position of his arms and legs to control the direction of his glide. Halfway down he was overtaken by a flight of paraso birds who flocked around him, playfully matching their speed with his, their long richly colored tails trailing behind them. Banking quickly for a sharp turn that would take him almost to the door of his nid-place, he surprised the drifting birds, causing a series of feather-ruffling collisions. As Raamo dropped to a stop on the wide branch that led to the door of his home, the birds swept upward and away, their soft giggling cries fading away into the forest's ever-present murmur of birdsong.

The nid-place of the D'ok family was in the upper midheights of the forest, and though not so large and impressive as those supported by lower and larger branches, it was roomy and comfortable. It consisted of a series of small chambers built in and around the crotch where several large grundbranches met. Like all other homes and buildings, its floors were constructed of the long straight trunks of rooftrees, and its walls were woven of frond and tendril and hung with decorated tapestries. As Raamo pushed aside the heavy door hanging, he heard his name called, and, turning, he saw his mother and sister climbing up the branchpath toward him.

"Raamo," his mother called. "How was it? What are you to be?"

"What are you to be?" There it was. The question asked of all young people after their Second Counseling, since it was then that the direction of their future lives was decided upon. Not that the decision usually came as a complete surprise. During their tenth and last year at the Garden, all students were consulted concerning their preferences. The Ol-zhaan, they were told, always took wishes as well as talents into consideration in the choosing of professions. But Raamo had approached his thirteenth year with no very strong leanings one way or another. He had thought he might be entered as an apprentice in the tapestry guild, since he had shown some slight talent for color and design. And there were times when he thought he might follow his father's profession of harvester, although he was not certain if his interest was actually in the work itself so much as in the element of adventure and mystery forever present in the lives of the orchard workers whose work took them daily so close to the forbidden floor of the forest. He would, of course, have liked to be as wise and learned as the teachers at the Garden, or even at the Academy, but he knew that was probably out of the question for someone with so faulty a memory. And, in moments of high and fanciful ambition, he had even considered the possibility of becoming a troubadour, one of those glamorous and highly admired individuals who spent their time traveling high and low through the seven cities of Green-sky, gathering news and information, which would then be sung to the populace from special platforms on the great public branchways.

But even in his wildest imaginings, Raamo had never even considered the possibility that he would be among the Chosen. And his family, he knew, would be as astounded as he.

"What are you to be?" his mother, Hearba, called again; and his little sister's thin piping, "What? What? What, Raamo?" trilled like the call of a bird. They reached him then, but before he could answer, there was the Palm

Song, or ceremony of greeting, to be chanted. Arms extended, he placed both palms against those of his mother and together they chanted the words of the greeting.

> *This our greeting, palm to palm,*
> *As our meeting fate-lines flow,*
> *Merged in Spirit and in song,*
> *Love and Joy united grow.*

He sang hurriedly, without giving thought to the meaning of the sacred words, in his haste to arrive at the telling of his astonishing news, and as he repeated the greeting with his sister, Pomma, he noticed that she did not even remember to look into his eyes. Instead her beautiful bluegreen eyes played over his face.

"What Raamo? What will you be?" she piped again the moment the greeting was finished. Watching her curiosity, Raamo was almost tempted to prolong the mystery of his future in order to enjoy the change he saw in her, brought on by the excitement of her only brother's Second Counseling.

Pomma was not often thus. Engrossed in private dreams, light boned and delicate as a bird, she spent most of her time drifting silently around the nid-place, her beloved pet, a tiny lavender sima, perched on her shoulder or dangling from her neck. She seldom took part in the games or dances of childhood and even made excuses to escape the daily excursions into the open forest to look for paraso tails and trencher beaks—excursions that were the delight, as well as the duty, of most Kindar children. Instead Pomma preferred to lie quietly on a secluded branch with her shuba floating around her so that sudden updrafts sometimes caught and lifted her several inches into the air. It was not often that she laughed, or even sang, except for the necessary rituals, and her pale skin had an unnatural translucency, as if light could penetrate her flesh as easily as it did the petals of a mistborne flower. The mistborne, a fragile blossom that drifted upward through the forest on damp days, its transparent petals immune to the weak gravity of Green-sky, often reminded Raamo of his sister, Pomma.

But today Pomma's cheeks glowed with life, and watching her, Raamo experienced his first moment of pure pleasure in the great honor that had come to him— pleasure at last unmixed with shock and anxiety.

"Aha, little Berry-dreamer," he teased. "So you are awake enough to be curious."

Pomma frowned shockingly, mindless of everything she had been carefully taught about unjoyful expressions in public places. "Don't call me that," she said. "I haven't had a single Berry all day."

Raamo smiled, knowing by pense that she was only pretending unjoyfulness toward him. Although she frowned, Pomma's thoughts were open to his pensing, and he read there only eager interest—and a kind of shocked anticipation, almost as if she already suspected— But how could she? He had been making a special effort not to mind-touch, and for many months now, Pomma had claimed that she could no longer pense, not even with members of her own family.

The ancient skill of pensing, or mind-touching, had once been practiced by people of all ages, but for many generations it had been lost to all except the very young. The skill usually faded between the ages of five and ten, and Pomma, at seven, had for several months claimed total inability. But now Raamo felt certain that, somehow, Pomma was very close to knowing his secret.

"Tricky one," he said. "You've been pensing. And you said you'd lost it."

"I had," she said. "I've not been able to for a long time, even with you. It must be just that I wanted to so badly. And it was only for a moment."

"What is it, daughter," their mother asked. "What did you pense? What is Raamo to be?"

"I don't know," Pomma said uncertainly. "I must have only imagined it. I imagined that he—" She stopped and stared at Raamo, her eyes enormous with wonder. "A— a—Chosen?" she stammered.

They both stared at her. The mother in shocked amazement, and Raamo in surprise that Pomma had really pensed him, that she had not lost the power after all.

"A Chosen?" Hearba said. Her eyes were wide with shock, but Raamo could pense no disbelief—and she did not chide Pomma for her mistaken pensing. It would seem that his mother found his incredible news easier to accept than Raamo had found it himself.

"Yes, Mother," he said. "I am a Chosen. It is to be told at the next assembly."

CHAPTER TWO

*I*t was the most perturbing evening of their lives. Sitting together in the common room of their comfortably familiar nid-place, the members of the D'ok family were, that night, lost in a suddenly unfamiliar world. A world where they experienced strange emotions and struggled to comprehend unthinkable ideas.

Watching them—seeing his father's shocked silence, his mother's restless and distant manner, and Pomma's unnatural wide-eyed intentness—Raamo pensed that for each there were moments of great Joy. But it seemed, for the most part, a strange unnatural Joy, arising from the mind and feeding on flamboyant imaginings rather than on warm and living moments of Peace and happiness. Trained as they were to seek and treasure simple daily Joys, the Kindar were ill prepared to deal with high excitements and the sudden glory of fame and honor.

The situation that the D'ok family was facing that evening was, indeed, a rare one. In all of Green-sky, in all the seven cities, and among all of its myriad citizens, only two were chosen each year to enter the temple. Only two out of hundreds.

No one in the D'ok family, certainly not Raamo himself, had any idea what it would be like to be an Ol-zhaan. The life of an Ol-zhaan was beyond the comprehension of ordinary citizens, beyond even their imaginings. Who, among the Kindar, could picture what it would be like to be a person of power and glory—a priest, magician, leader and healer? It was a thing far beyond understanding.

There was, however, one thing that Raamo and his family knew for certain. They knew that within a few short days every part of their lives would begin to change. Not only Raamo's life, but the others', also.

Very soon, Raamo had been told, the entire family would be required to move to a new nid-place on one of the grand lower branchpaths, among the families of grund-leaders, guildmasters, and other Kindar of high honor. For the next year, the Year of Honor, Raamo would continue to live at home, except for brief periods when he would be called to the temple or away to another city on one of the seven tours of honor. From time to time, during the year, the D'ok family would be required to accompany Raamo on a tour, or to appear with him at one of the great public celebrations of The Choosing, at which they would be honored and reverenced by all the Kindar.

What it would all be like, what such great changes would mean to them, they could not know. They knew only that change was coming, that it had already begun, and that in nine days' time there would be an assembly and an announcement, and after that the changes would be enormous and forever.

They had been sitting together in the common room

since late afternoon. The three of them—Raamo, Hearba and Pomma—had not been there long when the father, Valdo D'ok, arrived. Valdo's reaction to their news was, like everything else that day, strange and unexpected. A boisterous and talkative man, Valdo was immediately stricken with an unnatural speechlessness. Silent and unapproachable, he sat stiffly for a long time, making no sound except for an occasional burst of laughter or a long tremulous sigh.

The time for eating had come and gone and twilight had deepened into darkness before any one of the family recalled the time, and the activities left undone, and the rituals uncelebrated.

Roused at last from the stupor of thought by the hungry whimpering of Pomma's pet sima, Valdo D'ok gestured with astonishment at the darkening sky outside the window.

"Great Sorrow!" he exclaimed, using a term popular among harvesters, but considered indelicate by others. "Great Sorrow! Here it is nightfall, and we have not celebrated food-taking, nor even so much as set out the honey lamps. Here we sit staring into darkness like a tribe of Pash-shan."

They looked up at him smiling, his wife and daughter and the boy, Raamo, who had been his son for thirteen years but was soon to become something far beyond. They smiled with relief, grateful for being called back to the normal and expected, to the pleasant routines of life.

"I'll set the lamps, Father," Pomma said. Springing upward so lightly that she almost seemed to drift, she unhooked the cages of woven tendril from where they hung near the ceiling, and while her father placed the table-board and Raamo helped his mother bring food from the pantry, she quickly baited the lamps with fresh honey and set them outside the door of the nid-place. By the time the food was on the table, the lamps were full and glowing, each of them containing several moon-moths, fat round beetles whose phosphorescent bodies glowed with soft cool light. When the softly glowing lanterns were hung above the table, the ceremony of food-taking was begun.

"Now the Joy of tables laden," they began the Hymn of Food-taking. Their voices, blending in the intricate rhythms and harmonies, rose clear and sweet, and on this night as ever, infinitely pleasing to the ear and soothing to the mind. As they sang, they sought each other's eyes, smiling, and when the first verse was finished they did not stop, as was the common practice now except at official ceremonies and assemblies. In unison, as if by pensed signal, they continued on into the complicated and time-consuming second part of the Food-taking ritual—the dance and ceremonial sharing—and when they sat, at last, around the table, it was with full Peace and Joy. The pan was rich and tender; the fruit was sweet; and the egg sauce, light and tasty. They ate contentedly, their minds quiet and untroubled, their thoughts occupied for the moment only with the amusing antics of the sima, Baya.

Baya was trying to steal tidbits of food from the table. Although a full plate had been placed on her sleeping shelf, she preferred the excitement of snatching crumbs and rinds from the family's dishes. Creeping around the floor near their feet, the sly sima would from time to time raise herself on her hind legs until just the top half of her tiny wizened face, with its almost human purple eyes, would clear the edge of the table-board. With eyes wildly rolling, she would silently stretch out her long wisp of an arm, and the delicate handlike paw would close on an unprotected morsel. Then the tiny face, with its peering eyes, would disappear with miraculous suddenness and from beneath the table there would come small sounds of munching and smacking.

But when Valdo foiled a raid on his plate by lifting it suddenly out of reach, the sima reacted with loud chattering, baring her tiny teeth and pounding her long fingered paws on the table. Such an uncontrolled display of unjoyfulness by a creature so nearly human in appearance was just close enough to being indecent to seem wildly funny. The D'ok family's laughter was as limitless and unconstrained as that of Garden children in their first year of Joy.

"Ah," Valdo said contentedly, "we should take time to follow the full ritual more often. See how the old ways are still the best for bringing quietness to troubled minds."

There followed only silence, and the father, glancing around, realized that his statement had only served to remind the others of the troubling events of the day.

"And yet," the mother said quickly, "one hears so often that the old rituals and ceremonies are losing their power and becoming meaningless."

"Rumors," Valdo said loudly. "Only rumors. If one listens to rumors, one can hear many troubling things. Many things more troubling than anything that could be said about the simple rituals of ordinary Kindar."

Raamo laughed. "The harvesters are famous as rumor carriers," he said. "There is a saying that in the orchards, rumors grow faster than pan."

His father looked up quickly, and there was a sharp edge to his voice as he spoke. "Yes," he said, "I've heard that saying—and another truer one that says, 'Much can be seen under open skies.' Believe me, my lad, we harvesters see much that is hidden from the eyes of others."

"Like what, Father?" Pomma said. "I thought there were always Ol-zhaan Protectors in the orchards to make certain that the harvesters look only at their work, and especially," Pomma's voice trembled with vicarious alarm at the very thought, "—and especially not down at the forest floor. What have you seen that others haven't, Father?"

Valdo looked at his daughter uneasily, as if he wished he had been less outspoken, and when she pressed him further, he began to talk of other things—of the importance of the profession of harvester and of how, although they received little recognition or reward, the orchard workers were in many ways the most indispensable people in all Green-sky.

"I remember, at my own Second Counseling, all who were picked that year to become harvesters were taken to a special chamber, and there we were spoken to by the Ol-zhaan D'ol Falla, who is now the oldest and most honored of all the Ol-zhaan—"

"I think I saw her today," Raamo said. "She did not say her name, but I was examined by a woman Ol-zhaan of great age. I'm sure it was she."

Valdo shook his head decisively. "No," he said. "It is quite unlikely. D'ol Falla still leads the Vine Processions, but except for that she is rarely seen by ordinary Kindar. She is of much too great rank to spend her time at counsel."

"But what was it you were going to tell us," Hearba said, "concerning D'ol Falla's counsel for the harvesters?"

"Yes," Valdo said. "I was about to say that D'ol Falla told us that we were chosen as harvesters, not only for our strength of back and limb and our healthy vigor that we might withstand the fierce heat of the orchards where there are no rooftrees to shield against the sun's rays, but also, and most important, we were chosen for our steadfastness of mind and Spirit. Only those, she said, with unusual firmness of mind, ungiven to flights of fancy, were suited for such dangerous and important work. D'ol Falla herself said it. And it is true. It is not for the timid hearted to work where the tunnels of the Pash-shan run everywhere just below the Root, so that their growls and cries can often be heard and one must always keep one's eyes averted to avoid the enchantment of their evil eyes."

As Valdo's voice rolled and swelled, his wife and children listened attentively, although they had heard much before concerning the life of the orchard workers. None of them had ever been past the orchard boundaries, beyond which only the trained harvesters were permitted to go; but they knew well, from Valdo's stories, exactly what it was like. They could picture almost as clearly as if they could still play the childhood game of Five-Pense—a game in which young children pensed visual images to each other—exactly how it looked in the great open areas. Areas where, long ago, the forest had been cleared of sheltering rooftrees and giant grunds, so that the hot rays of the sun could shine down on the produce trees that thrived in the bright sunlight. These trees, much smaller than grunds but still towering many hundreds of feet into the brilliant skies, produced many varieties of fruits and nuts as well as the all-important pan, the heavy full-bodied fruit that was the staple of the Green-sky diet. And they also knew, very well, exactly how and why the ever-present danger of the Pash-shan was so much greater in the orchards than elsewhere in Green-sky.

Every child of the Kindar began to learn about the Pash-shan in earliest infancy. From the time a child learned to climb from his nid and crawl about the floor of his home and out onto the branchpaths, he was constantly being cautioned about the Pash-shan. Indeed, it was then, before a child was old enough to wear and use a shuba, that the Pash-shan were the greatest threat—because it was only then that falling was a real and constant danger. Not from the fall itself, since the gentle gravity of Green-sky was not apt to cause serious injury unless one fell from the very highest regions. But a fall that ended on the forest floor put anyone, child or adult, in grave and terrible danger—because there, on the dark fern-choked earth, far below the great pathways formed by the lower branches of the grundtrees, the Pash-shan were very, very near.

Almost no one among the Kindar had ever seen a Pash-shan, except in restless dreams or evil imaginings, but every Kindar knew exactly what they looked like and how they came to be imprisoned beneath the surface of the earth. In their homes as well as in the classes at the Garden, Kindar children learned by memory how the Ol-zhaan, far back in the days of the flight, had, through the Spirit-force of ritual and ceremony and the ancient skill of grunspreking, changed a strong native vine into the Wissenvine—the Sacred Ivy, builder, comforter and protector of all human life on Green-sky. Not only did the Vine produce the soothing Berry used in ritual and ceremony, as well as at times of unjoyfulness and stress, but its long limber tendrils were used in almost every form of construction. Everything, every structure, every article of furniture, nearly every utensil used by the Kindar, was fashioned at least in part from tendrils. Limber and elastic when alive, when severed from the Vine, the slender tendrils hardened quickly to a material of almost indestructible toughness and strength. Thus a nid, a womblike cradling hammock, was woven of springy living tendril, while thicker ones, severed and shaped, could support a table-board or frame a wall.

But as necessary as were the Berries and tendrils of the Vine, they were as nothing compared to the indispensable protection given by the Root. The Root of the Wissenvine was an enchanted growth. Summoned and nurtured by grunspreking—the ancient art of Spirit-force communication with plant life—the Holy Root spread over the entire surface of Green-sky in a close-woven latticework of indestructible strength. And below this lattice in their dark and noisome caverns lived the soul-eating, cloud-spinning monsters, the fearful dream-haunting Pash-shan.

All these things the Kindar learned in infancy, but according to Valdo, there were other facts concerning the Pash-shan known only to the harvesters.

"In the forest," Valdo told his family, as he had often told them before, "the tunnels run far below the surface of the earth and only rarely approach the surface, while in the orchards the Pash-shan have dug many tunnels that run in every direction, just below the grillwork of Wissen-root. Do you know why it is that they have done this?"

"Yes, father. To steal food and try to catch harvesters," Pomma answered, but Valdo explained anyway, in case she was not really certain or had forgotten an important detail.

"The surface tunnels in the forest are used only for ventilation and, of course, as lookouts for fallen Kindar foolish or unlucky enough to be within reach of their long arms and sharp claws."

"What happens to them—the fallen Kindar?" Pomma asked, her face puckered with fascinated horror, intrigued in spite of herself by this part of the recital.

"Who knows. Eaten undoubtedly. Perhaps sliced to bits by the long claws."

"Valdo, please," Hearba said. "It's not decent to speak of such things. Particularly before children."

"Except they don't eat the babies who fall," Pomma prompted her father.

"We know only that they don't eat all of them," he agreed. "Babies small enough to be pulled down through an opening in the Root are kept alive—as slaves. It is well known that there are Kindar slaves in the lower regions. Kidnappers, the Pash-shan are, as well as thieves who lie in wait constantly in their orchard ditches, trying to catch every morsel of fruit or pan that falls from the trees before it can be harvested."

"But you spoke of rumors," Hearba said. "Of whispers spreading among the harvesters. What do they concern?"

Valdo's brow contracted into furrows as his thoughts shifted with apparent reluctance from solid certainties to troubling suspicions. "Only rumors," he said again, but with less assurance. "There are some who say that the cloud columns of the Pash-shan rise daily from new locations, and that this is undoubtedly the cause of the increase in illness and mind-pain among the Kindar. And there is also talk concerning the great increase in the number of Vine Processions, of late. Almost every day in recent weeks, one sees processions of Vine Priests bearing the urns and symbols and the great altar of Wissen, on their way to the forest floor. There are those who say that all is not well with the Blessed Vine—that there are places where the Root seems to be withering and the spaces between growing larger and more open. That is what they are saying but it is perhaps, only talk, with no meaning."

"At the last assembly," Raamo said, "the Ol-zhaan spoke of the need to return to the old ways and practice the ceremonies more faithfully. Perhaps the Ol-zhaan are only setting a good example. Perhaps in the olden days the processions were always made more often."

"Exactly," Valdo said. "I mentioned the same thing last week when some of the rumor spreaders were whispering in the robing room as I was putting on my shading garments. I said that it was probably only a return to the old ways, but they said—" Valdo paused suddenly, uneasily.

"And they said?" Raamo urged.

"That there have been more disappearances lately. That among the missing have been grown men and women, some of high honor, and that it is almost certain that they have been taken by the Pash-shan."

"But how?" Pomma asked. "They surely couldn't have fallen—"

"Not unless they carelessly ventured out of their nid-places without their shubas," her father said. "It seems unlikely that grown men and women, among them learned academicians and high officials, would do anything so foolish, but perhaps they did. Unless they were even more foolish, and ventured down to the forest floor of their own free will."

"Surely no one would do that," Raamo said.

"It is hard to believe," his father said. "But I'd rather believe that than—" Again he paused and then went on hurriedly. In his agitation his thoughts broke through the careful mind-blocking that was a part of his very nature, and Raamo was able to pense that he was deeply troubled. "—than what they are whispering. That the Root is, indeed, withering and that there are places where the Pash-shan have already broken through into Green-sky."

They stared at him in consternation as, with obvious effort, Valdo D'ok regained his composure—and with it the mental barrier that usually so effectively checked the sending of his true thoughts and feelings. He smiled stiffly, and the words he gave them were cheerful and comforting. "But, of course, there can be no truth in such rumors, or the Ol-zhaan would have told us so."

They smiled in return, Raamo and Hearba and the wide-eyed Pomma, and silence fell among them. Outside the nid-place the night rains had begun and the falling droplets rustled in the rooffronds and whispered down the broad surfaces of the grundleaves. The damp forest air, fragrant with greening life, breathed through the loosely woven walls. Somewhere nearby a flock of paraso birds giggled sleepily, and from the distance came the occasional shriek of a blue-winged trencher. The sima whimpered softly and climbed into Pomma's lap. Clinging to the soft folds of the child's shuba, she turned her nearly human face from side to side, as though listening to sounds that only she could hear.

In their woven cages the moonmoths grew dimmer, and at last Hearba rose and lifted her palms to Raamo's in the tender ritual of parting.

"Good night, my Raamo," she said, and then smiling almost teasingly, "my Chosen one."

"I'd almost forgotten," he said.

"Yes, yes," Valdo broke in heartily. "Your mother is

right. It is very late. The time for sleeping will soon be over."

But hours later, swaying gently in his nid, the time for sleeping still had not come for Raamo. Although soothed by the rocking nid and the breathing, flowing night, his mind refused to accept the comfort of sleep. Instead it raced on and on, exploring and questioning. It was truly the strangest night of his life.

CHAPTER THREE

He slept briefly. When he awakened, the night rains were scarcely over and, on every leaf and frond, drops still gathered, clung, and then fell slowly down through the sweet green damp of the forest morning. Slanting rays of early sun, filtering through the rooffronds, made channels of light in which the falling drops were turned into sparkling stars. Leaning out the window, Raamo had a sudden wish to leap outward and drift down a corridor of sunlight, splashing through the glittering stardrops and spattering them into a million smaller stars that would trail behind him in sheets and plumes of brilliance as he glided down, down—

Finding himself perched precariously on the window ledge, in nothing but his waistcloth, Raamo slid back to the floor of his nid-room, and quickly slipped into his shuba, fastening the wrist and ankle straps securely before he returned to the window. The raindrops had nearly stopped, but now Raamo noticed that just above his window a Wissenflower had blossomed during the night. It was an enormous bloom, its thick translucent petals glowing, flowing, with changing shades of rich deep reds and purples and tender fruity oranges and ambers. Breathing the tantalizing fragrance, Raamo was tempted to touch or even taste the petals, as he had often tried to do as a young child. He had tried many times before he gave up, resigned at last to the sad reality that a Wissenflower could not be tasted or touched without causing it to wither immediately to ragged grayish shreds.

Extending both arms toward the Flower, Raamo centered the force of his Spirit into his fingertips and concentrated—narrowing and channeling all his body energy until he could feel it flowing out toward the loop of Vine that bore the Sacred Bloom. The tingling in his fingertips grew stronger, and the Vine began to move closer until the Flower was only inches from his face. Still holding the looped Vine by the force of kiniporting, Raamo drank in the beauty of the pulsing colors and breathed deeply of the intoxicating odors. But as his face approached the edge of a petal it recoiled, thickening and shortening as it drew away from him, back into the center of the Bloom.

"Raamo," his mother's voice startled him, and as his Spirit-force wavered, the loop of Wissenvine straightened, pulling the Blossom upward and away. Hearba came to the window and stood beside him looking up at the glorious Blossom.

"How lovely it is," she said, "and how sad that it dies so easily." She smiled at Raamo. "I see that you are still able to kiniport."

"Yes, a little. I can lift things of little weight or substance, and move them toward me, but that is all. Nothing out of the ordinary."

"Nothing out of the ordinary?" Hearba questioned.

"Do you mean you know others of your age who can do as much?"

"Why yes," Raamo said. "In my last year of kiniport at the Garden there were many who could move the cylinders more rapidly than I."

"Truly?" Hearba asked. "I had thought—" She paused and then continued. "But Pomma told me that she believes that no one in her class can truly kiniport anymore. And even when I was a child in the Garden, most of my classmates could no longer lift or summon so much as a feather by the time they were nine or ten years old."

Raamo was puzzled. "But I have seen them kiniporting, and not long ago. The children in Pomma's class and even older ones."

"Pomma told me—only last month when she brought home her latest reports—that she could no longer kiniport except by illusion. I had praised her for her good mark in kiniporting, and she giggled dreamily—I think she had been eating Berries on the way home—and said she should have gotten failing in kiniporting and excellent in illusion. She said she was really very good at illusion."

"Illusion?" Raamo asked. "What did she mean?"

"I asked her, of course, and she seemed, for a moment, worried that she had told, but then she giggled again and said, 'All right, I'll tell you.' And she told me that two or three years ago when she began to be unable to move the cylinders by Spirit-force, one of the teachers kept her in after class and showed her how the tables were hung and balanced so that a touch of knee or elbow would set them vibrating in such a way that the cylinders began to move toward the end of the table where the one stood who was practicing—or pretending to practice— kiniporting.

"And after that, she said, she watched the others closely and saw that most of them were vibrating the tables also. She said that she had become very good at causing the table to vibrate in a manner that was very difficult to detect, and that the teacher praised her for it and said that when one loses Spirit-force one must learn illusion to take its place. She also said that there are ways of practicing illusion in the pensing class and that her good mark in pensing was also due to the use of illusion."

Raamo shook his head disbelievingly. "But if all, or most, of the children were not able to pense or kiniport, and if the teachers were telling everybody else about this—this illusion—why is it that I didn't know? I realize that most people lose the Spirit-force. But to such an extent—so soon. Surely someone would have told me."

"Perhaps," Hearba said, "the teachers did not tell you since you were still able to practice the Spirit-arts truly, and therefore there was no need for them to teach you false ways. And the other children might not have told you because of shame. Pomma said the teacher who spoke to her told her that it was a great disgrace to lose the Spirit-skills at such an early age—that none of her classmates had yet lost them—and that she was being taught about the art of illusion in order to hide her disgrace. The teacher said she should not speak of the matter to anyone—not even her own family." Hearba paused. "But I do think it strange that you did not learn the truth by pensing."

Raamo nodded slowly. "I think I know—" he said. "I often wondered why everyone mind-blocked so carefully during kiniporting class. And during pensing it always seemed to me that everyone was mind-blocking much more than at other times. I always found it harder to pense in class than at other times. I often wondered why."

"How are the pensing classes conducted now?" Hearba asked. "Is it still by image-sending?"

"Yes. Almost entirely. The sender and receiver sit in separate screened booths, with several familiar objects on the table in front of them. The sender opens his mind to one object only and the receiver, if he can pense what the object is, sets the same thing from his table in the booth window—behind a curtain. Then the sender tells the examiner what object he was sending—and the curtain is opened to see if the pensing was correct."

"Is there time," Hearba asked, "to change the object in the window—after the sender tells what it was that he was sending?"

"I—I suppose there would be," Raamo said. "I had never thought—but yes, there might be time."

There was a silence while Raamo and his mother stood by the window together, and yet alone in their separate thoughts. A trencher bird flew by, the early sunlight burnishing the iridescent blue of its scaly wings. It was carrying a large breadnut in its enormous beak, and Raamo leaned out the window eagerly trying to determine the direction of its nest. The beak had been dark in color, suggesting that it would soon be shed and that its huge, tightly woven nest might contain other discarded beaks as well—a treasure chest of sharp blades to be used in every kind of cutting tool from fruit knife to wood chisel. To seek out trencher nests with their harvests of indispensable blades was the task of every Kindar child old enough to climb or glide.

"I think I know the grund he's headed for," Raamo began excitedly. "This afternoon I'll get Bruvo to help me, and I'll—" He stopped suddenly, as the remembrance came to him that he was no longer a carefree child with no more pressing duty than the seeking out of trencher nests. He glanced at Hearba and saw on her face an expression he had not seen before. She seemed to be regarding him, her own son, with a kind of wonder. Turning his mind to hers, he found that she was not blocking and that her thoughts were clear to him—if puzzling. She was thinking of how she had long suspected that he might be destined for a high calling.

"I never knew you thought such things of me," he said. "I always thought I was only—"

"I took care that you should not know," Hearba said. "Mothers are often wrong about such things, and I would not have wished to fill your head with grand ideas and false ambitions."

"But these things of which we have been speaking, pensing and kiniporting, do not explain the choosing," Raamo said. "Surely an Ol-zhaan is not chosen on the strength of his ability at such children's games."

"The Spirit-skills are more than children's games," Hearba said. "They are—they are the branchway to holiness. Surely the Spirit Hymn is still sung every morning in the Garden?" Hearba began to sing softly, and Raamo blended his voice with hers.

> *"Spirit-gift is the glory of Kindar birth.*
> *Spirit-force is the seventh and highest sense.*
> *The Spirit-skills are the branchway to holiness.*
> *Spirit is the All-in-One."*

When the blending tones of the last, long drawn-out syllable had died away Raamo said, "Yes, of course, the

Hymn is still sung. But what does it mean? The teachers lead us in the singing of the Spirit Hymn every morning, but when I asked them to explain its meaning, they said but little."

Hearba nodded. "Little was said concerning it even when I was a student in the Garden. But there is an old saying that goes, 'As the orchard nourishes the pan-tree, so does Spirit grow in the Garden.' I have heard that in the olden days much more emphasis was placed on the importance of the Spirit-skills. And who knows, perhaps even today it is important and the new Ol-zhaan must be chosen from among those who show unusual Spirit-gift as infants. Perhaps such early skills *are* in some way related to the great powers of an Ol-zhaan."

"Perhaps," Raamo said, "but still, I don't understand—"

At that moment his words were interrupted by Pomma's voice shrilling, "Baya! Baya! Come back here. Drop that."

The sima burst through the door hangings and scuttled across the floor of Raamo's chamber carrying a small gathered bag in one of her front paws. Pomma was close behind, but before she could catch her pet it had leaped to the window ledge and tossed the bag away. Pomma grabbed for it and missed. Leaning out, she watched it fall slowly down and down toward the forest floor.

"Oh, Baya!" she cried, her face contorted. "I'm going to—I'd like to—*dead* you!"

"Pomma," Hearba's voice reflected her shocked amazement. "Where did you learn such language? Go to your chamber at once and chant the Hymn of Peace until you are ready to speak decently."

Raamo was a bit shocked himself. Even among older

children such a curse word was not commonly used. The word "dead," while perfectly acceptable as an adjective describing the condition of not being alive, when used as a verb meaning the taking of life was officially a non-word, and therefore carefully avoided.

Pomma stood facing her mother for a moment breathing deeply, her small body clad only in a short waistcloth, trembling with every breath. Then she hung her head and turned to go.

"Pomma," Hearba called after her, "what was in the bag that was important enough to make you so forget yourself?"

Without turning Pomma answered, her voice low and trembly. "It was Berries," she said. "It was all of my Berries."

When Pomma was gone and the heavy doorway tapestry had fallen into place behind her, Raamo said, "She eats too many Berries, Mother. Can't you explain to her that she is too young to need so much mind-soothing. She should be out climbing and gliding and dancing instead of Berry-dreaming on some lonely branch. Did you see, Mother, how thin she is and how the light shines through her fingers as if they had no more substance than the wings of a silk-moth?"

Hearba nodded, sighing. "I have tried," she said. "But with the Berry so plentiful, and so much encouragement—in the Gardens and elsewhere. Pomma says that some of the teachers distribute Berries in the classroom when the children become noisy or restless. Even in their songs there is encouragement—so much praise of the Berry and its happy dreams. It seems that in recent years the Berry-songs are the most popular of any, among the children." Hearba sighed again. "I have been thinking of taking Pomma to the next assembly of healing."

Raamo bent to pick up the sima who had been sitting at his feet, looking up at him and tugging at his shuba. Cradled in his arms, the little creature looked anxiously up into Raamo's face as he asked, "Do you think, then, that it is more than just the Berry-eating? Do you think that she is really ill?"

"I don't know," Hearba answered. "But I am troubled that it may be so."

Illness of any kind was rare in Green-sky, and there were no minor illnesses, so Raamo's mind was darkened by his mother's words.

In his arms the sima's tiny lavender face contorted as if in pain, and it rocked itself to and fro, wailing softly, as if it understood their words and was troubled with them.

CHAPTER FOUR

*T*he day had started poorly, with Pomma's outburst, but by the time the ceremony of the new day had been completed, the solace of song and the release of meditation, along with the natural Kindar tendency to hopefulness and good cheer, had worked their magic, and the D'ok family was at Peace. Pomma no longer pouted, and Raamo and his mother had freed their minds, at least for the moment, from the shadow of worry. Immediately after the morning food-taking, Valdo took his leave, since the day of a harvester began very early. Even in their head shades and protective shubas, the strength of the midday sun in the orchards was oppressive to the forest-bred Kindar, so they were forced to begin their work early and to rest during the hours of high sun. More than an hour later Hearba, Raamo, and Pomma left their nid-place together, on their way to separate destinations.

Raamo was on his way to Temple-grove, a stand of exceptionally large grunds on the northern boundary of the central city of Orbora. It was there that the Ol-zhaan lived, in lavish chambers among great palaces and temples, and it was there that he had been told to come on the morning after his Second Counseling. He had not been told why or what he was to do there, but only that he should wait in one of the smaller reception halls until he received further instructions.

Hearba was on her way to her place of work in the silkhouses where she did print embroidery, and where her days were spent in alternating hours of work and social communion—song, dance, and conversation— with other members of the silk guild, with spinners, weavers and keepers of worm and moth.

They would stop first, however, at the Garden of Song and Story, where Pomma, along with every other child in the city between the ages of two and twelve, would spend her day.

Although their destinations were different, they began their journey together, and in the same way. Not far from the dooryard of their own nid-place, a large branchfork, unhampered by the trunks of rooftrees or curtains of Wissenvine, offered a perfect launching spot for long glides. It was there that Hearba first, and then her two children, leaned forward into the open air, hundreds of feet above the forest floor, and began to fall. By stretching their arms and legs wide, they tightened the flowing wing-panels of their shubas into taut sails that caught the air and buoyed them up. After the initial sharp plunge, their descent was gradual, and they swooped and banked, and at times even soared briefly upward as they were caught by sudden updrafts of warm damp air.

Dropping down past great networks of Vine and grundbranches of ever-increasing size, they at last reached the lower regions where, along the enormous public branchways, were to be found not only the large nid-places of high officials but also the great public buildings and assembly halls. Banking in unison, like a formation of large birds, the D'ok family skirted a gigantic grundtrunk, festooned with dozens of Vine-woven ladders, and dropped lightly to a landing in the public dooryard of the Garden.

On each side the branchpaths were thick with Kindar hurrying toward the Garden, and others glided in constantly to land nearby. Parents of infants in their first year at the Garden arrived either walking or gliding, with their offspring strapped to their backs—as they would have to do until the Garden teachers certified their children as proficient in the use of the shuba and capable of gliding on their own. Large groups of older children arrived together, singing and shouting as they ran along the branches or swooped down from the heights. Touching palms briefly with her mother and brother, and chattering a few disjointed words of the parting, Pomma dashed away after a group of her fifth-year classmates, who were just disappearing behind the door hangings of the main entrance. She turned once to wave, a quick birdlike gesture, the rich color of her bluegreen eyes in striking contrast to her small pale face, and then using both her tiny hands to push aside the heavy draperies, she, too, disappeared. For several moments Raamo and Hearba stood watching the dwindling flow of students as the time approached for the beginning of the morning's classes.

Raamo was thinking of his own days at the Garden, which had ended such a short time before, but which seemed now to be already fading into a distant past.

Like all other Kindar children, he had begun to attend

the Garden classes at the end of his second year of life, and by the time he reached his third birthday he had been taught many things. He had learned, of course, to wear a shuba and to glide, so that he no longer needed to be watched and guarded every moment to prevent a tragic fall to the forest floor; but also he had begun to receive instruction in many other areas of study.

Already, in that first year, he had begun classes in Love, where he was encouraged to relate to his fellow students by playing games that emphasized cooperation and shared achievement, and the delight of shared emotions. In Peace class he was taught how to control and make positive use of his emotions by using ritual and meditation; and in his first year of Joy, he had learned to appreciate not only the pleasures of song and dance but the many other delights of body, mind, and Spirit.

He had also begun instructions designed to increase and prolong his use of Spirit-force, and in a daily class known as Story, he had been taught to recite by memory the chants and songs and narrations that told the history of Green-sky.

But memorization, so necessary for Kindar children, had always been hard for Raamo. It was with difficulty that he had learned not only the long sacred stories but also the songs and chants used in the many rituals and ceremonies of daily life. He had often been chided by his teachers, who told him that he could easily do better if he would only try—that there was nothing really wrong with his memory if only he would spend more time remembering and less at asking pointless questions and daydreaming about strange and disquieting ideas. "You are as curious as a sima," his teachers had told him, "and almost as destructive." That had been the time he had almost spoiled a book by trying to write on one of its pages with various juices squeezed from fruits and tree bark. He had been trying to find a way to produce books more quickly and easily so they would be more plentiful. "But such books could never be as beautiful as embroidered ones," his teachers had said—and it was true.

Books, with their pages of finely woven silk, illustrated and printed in bright colored thread, stitched by the most talented embroiderers, were indeed beautiful—and immensely valuable and rare. Of course, they could only be owned by schools and temples. All other writing was very temporary, since it was done by stylus on grundleaves, and grundleaves tended to dry and disintegrate in a very short time.

"But everyone should have books of their own," Raamo had said, "in their own chambers. Then they could have many stories and histories to read at any time and—"

"But what need to read history when it is already written in your mind?" his teacher had asked. "And it is written in the minds of all Kindar who have studied carefully and have memorized the ancient songs and stories during their days at the Garden. Study hard, Raamo, and you will have no need of books of your own." But Raamo had continued to have trouble with his memory, and his reports were not often very high.

He had usually done somewhat better in the Spirit-skill classes. He had always been given high marks in those classes, although it had seemed to him that many among his classmates pensed more accurately and kiniported with less effort. But that, he remembered suddenly, might have been at least partly, and perhaps almost entirely, due to illusion.

"I wonder," he said to his mother, "do you think that the use of illusion is taught also in the classes in grunspreking?"

"Perhaps," she said, "although I don't see how—"

"I do," Raamo interrupted suddenly. "Now, I do."

Grunspreking, or the influencing of plant life by Spirit-force, was considered one of the most important of the Spirit-skills, since it was the grunspreking of the early Ol-zhaan, D'ol Wissen, that had saved Green-sky from the Pash-shan. In the Garden classes, Kindar children practiced grunspreking by trying to influence the growth of Vine-tendrils, making them divide into a certain number of finger tendrils and twine themselves into given patterns. After many days of ritual, meditation and plant-pensing, the pupil reported to his teacher how his tendril had grown—and exactly what he had asked of it.

"We were never asked to reveal what we had directed our tendrils to do until the end," Raamo told Hearba. "And then, if the shoot leaned to the left and sent out three feelers, it would be easy to say—"

"That you had so intended—" his mother finished. "And if the shoot sickened and withered away, one could even say one had willed it so," she added, smiling wryly. Then her smile faded, and she continued, "My mind is pained, Raamo, by this matter of the teaching of illusion instead of the true Spirit-skills. I don't know why exactly, but it is so. I wish—" her smile teased gently, "I wish that you were already an Ol-zhaan, full of wisdom and knowledge, so that I could ask your counsel in this matter."

"And I would counsel you," Raamo teased in return, "to eat five sacred Berries and retire to a private place and chant the Hymn of Peace until your mind-pain had healed itself."

"Would you, indeed?" Hearba said. "Such counsel I need not wait for." She turned and started off along the branchpath toward the silkhouses. "Come, Raamo," she called. "Walk with me as far as the crossbranch near the silkhouses. It will take no longer if you climb by way of Broadtrunk to the midheights and then cross over into Stargrund."

So Raamo accompanied his mother to the part of the city where, in long hallways, silkworms were fed and nurtured and silk was woven into many materials, from the light firm silk used for book pages and shubas, to the heavy weaves necessary for tapestries and door hangings—and then, in other hallways embroidered, not only with colored thread, but also with long iridescent strands from the plumes of paraso birds. They said their parting outside the door to the first embroidery hall, and Raamo continued alone toward the Temple-grove.

He walked quickly now, until he reached an enormous tree in the very center of the city. Broadgrund, as it was called, supported in its lower branches many shops and business houses, as well as the largest assembly hall in the city of Orbora. The trunk of Broadgrund was so wide that a hundred Kindar with arms outstretched could not have reached around it. Strung with dozens of Vine ladders, Broadtrunk was a central route to the upper reaches of the city, and on this morning, as always, it was crowded with climbers who, like Raamo, were on their way upward. At the moment, the upward flow was somewhat impeded by a group of deliverymen climbing downward carrying on their backs large bundles of produce. Too heavily laden to risk gliding, they were forced to make use of the ladders to reach the shops on the main branchways.

Struggling around and over the downward traffic, Raamo finally reached a midheight branchpath that led in the direction of Temple-grove. Surefooted and delicately balanced, like all Kindar, he ran lightly along the narrowing branch until he arrived at the spot where it paralleled a corresponding branch from the next grund. This was Stargrund, the first of the towering giants that made up the grove of the Ol-zhaan. From Stargrund a ramp, woven of Vine and branch, led upward to a central platform. Almost at the beginning of the ramp, Raamo stopped suddenly and then hurriedly stepped aside into a small branchfork.

A procession was approaching, making its way with full pomp and splendor, down the gently swaying rampway. It was, Raamo saw at once, a Vine-procession—a pilgrimage to the Vine, bearing the holy altar and symbol—on its way to the forest floor.

The procession consisted of nine Ol-zhaan, their pure white shubas glinting beneath the brilliance of feathered hoods and capes. The first two were carrying large lutes, and from their flowing fingers came the familiar strains of the solemn Vine-song. Behind them came bearers of urns and banners, and then four who bore on their shoulders the sacred Wissenaltar, a tendril-woven platform draped in tapestries so richly decorated that they dazzled the eyes of the beholder. Last came one alone, the famed D'ol Falla, the oldest and most honored of Ol-zhaan and high priestess of the Vine. She was dressed in a feathered cape woven entirely of the deep green neck-feathers of the male paraso, and she carried a long staff surmounted with the symbol of her high calling—a Wissenflower shaped of some magical material that gleamed hard and golden in the slanting rays of the sun. As the procession passed, very close to Raamo's refuge on the branchfork, he saw her face and knew that it had, indeed, been the great D'ol Falla who had spoken to him alone, at the time of his counseling.

Caught up in wonder at the beauty and magnificence of the procession, Raamo followed beside it, making his way frantically through scratchy twig clusters and enfolding grundleaves. But when the procession reached Startrunk and started down the ladders there, he was forced to stop. As the last Ol-zhaan disappeared from view, Raamo sighed—and then smiled, realizing that he had been marching with them in imagination, sharing in their splendor and glory. "It will take many years," he told himself, "many years and who knows what trials and testings before you can hope to be as one of those." It was a sobering thought—for a new Chosen who a moment before had been scrambling through branchends like an excited sima. Raamo brushed the twigs and tree ants out of his hair and again started up the ramp, walking this time with what he hoped was appropriate dignity. But then an even more sobering thought stopped him in midstride. He stood stiffly, as if stricken by paralysis at a sudden transition from Joy to fear. From his delight and Joy in the splendor of the procession, to his sudden fear for what it might mean.

"There have been many processions of late—" his father had said. "There are those who say the Root is withering—"

For long moments Raamo stood in the middle of the temple ramp while his mind troubled him with pictures of the glorious Ol-zhaan winding their way on and on, down ramps and then ladders, down and down to the dark deep undergrowth of the forest floor—the forest floor where no Kindar ever went, and where only the Root protected the brave Ol-zhaan from the monstrous inhabitants of the lower regions. And if the Root were truly withering?

CHAPTER FIVE

At the end of the Stargrund ramp, an enormous
arch hung with ancient tapestries marked the
beginning of the temple grounds. Inside the
gateway, a large open platform was surrounded on all
sides by other ramps and archways leading to many
chambers of great size and magnificence, supported by
the unusually large and level branches of the temple
grunds. Raamo crossed the open platform and entered the
first large chamber. This far he had been before, as had all
the citizens of Orbora, since this was the central Hall of
Counseling. Here he had sat, only the morning before,
with many other thirteen-year-olds, all of them waiting to
be led to smaller chambers where they would learn what
profession had been assigned to them and, therefore, the
general course and direction of their future lives. For all
of them, it had been a day of momentous importance—a
crossroads, an ending and a new beginning. A day to be
followed by great rejoicing or, in some cases, by bitter
disappointment.

Of course, any apprentice who was unsatisfied with
his assignment was free to request that he be given a new

profession. The teachers at the Garden had said so, and many people had heard of such a thing happening somewhere. However, Raamo had never met anyone who had changed his profession from the one given him on his Second Counseling, nor had anyone that he knew. So Raamo and his friends had each approached his Counseling knowing that it would be a day of unequaled significance. A day that quite possibly would change his entire life.

Today the great hall was empty and quiet, whereas yesterday it had been packed with anxious troubling thirteen-year-olds. As often happened in times of high emotion, particularly among the young, there was much imperfect or partial mind-blocking, so Raamo had been able to pense bits and pieces of many interesting, and sometimes surprising, hopes and fears. He had in fact been so caught up in pensing, his energy so channeled into what children called "pense-peeking," the receiving of unsent thought, that he had not yet begun to trouble about his own future—until a novice Ol-zhaan in a green tabard stepped into the hall and called his name. And Raamo had risen and walked across the room—and into a new existence.

Reliving it in his mind the next few hours, Raamo found himself shaking, pulsing with the same strange sensations that had troubled him for a time the day before. Sitting down quickly, he closed his eyes and began to mind-speak one of his favorites hymns of Peace. The soothing words were just beginning to have some effect when, from very near, a voice said, "Greetings, friend. Are you meditating or Berry-dreaming?"

Raamo's eyes flew open. Standing before him was a girl of about his own age. She was tall for a girl but delicately built, and her eyes were dark and had a level steadiness more natural to one of much greater age and honor. Either in the tone of her voice, or by a momentary pensing, Raamo was sure he read an intent to tease behind her question, as if she found it amusing that he had need of soothing.

"Neither," he said quickly, and then added, belatedly, the proper salutation for a stranger. "Greetings, friend, and welcome."

The girl nodded. She was indeed a stranger. She had certainly never been among the pupils at the Orbora Garden.

"You are not from Orbora, I think?" Raamo asked.

"No," she said. "I am Genaa D'anhk, and my nid-place is in Farvald. I am here to see—to speak with one of the Orbora Ol-zhaan."

Raamo tried not to stare in fascination, but it was not easy. He knew that, ordinarily, Garden graduates from the other cities did not come to Orbora for counseling. Then too, the girl was not mind-blocking completely enough to keep him from pensing that under the outward appearance of calm she was at least somewhat excited. It seemed possible, even likely, that she was the other Chosen.

"Are you—here for counseling?" he asked.

"No," she said. "I was counseled two days ago, in Farvald. I was—asked to come here to the temple for—further instructions."

It was apparent that she did not intend to speak further of the matter. Raamo remembered that he, too, had been asked to say nothing of his choosing except to members of his own family, until after the announcing.

"I am Raamo D'ok," Raamo told her. "I live here in Orbora. I too am awaiting a meeting with an Ol-zhaan."

The girl, Genaa, looked at him quickly, and it seemed to Raamo that her eyes flared with an intense probing light. "You're the other one," she said, suddenly. "You are also a Chosen?"

Startled by the directness of her question, Raamo momentarily forgot his promise of silence—enough to nod. "But I was told not to speak of it until after the announcing," he added quickly. "Did you pense me?"

Genaa shrugged, smiling. "Of course not," she said. "I haven't been able to pense in years. Except with someone who is sending intentionally—and very strongly. And not always, even then. It was only a logical guess. We are here together—only two of us. And I know why I'm here."

"I suppose it's all right for us to speak of it—since we are both—" Raamo paused, glancing toward the inner doorway.

"Of course," Genaa said. "If they had not wanted us to speak together, they would not have allowed us to meet here. What did they tell you—at your counseling?"

"Very little," Raamo said. "Only that I was—that I was to be a Chosen. And that I should tell my family and no one else until after the next assembly when the announcing will be made."

"And I also," the girl said. "And that I should travel as far as Ninegrund yesterday and stay the night there in the travelers' hall, and then come on to Orbora this morning."

"You must be very tired," Raamo said. "That is a long journey. To make it in so short a time, you must have—"

"I am very strong," Genaa interrupted. "I do not tire easily."

She looked strong, Raamo thought. In spite of the narrow grace of her body and the girl-child softness of her features, there was a strength and sureness about her.

"Did they tell you why?" he asked. "Did they say why you were chosen?"

"No," she said. "Why? Did they tell you?"

"No," Raamo said. "It was just that I wondered—that I've been wondering about it. About why they picked me." As he spoke it came flooding back—the shock of it, the disbelief.

Genaa's stare was frankly curious, and he realized that he had let his face reflect the reliving of his turmoil. He smiled, shrugging. "It's only that it was such a surprise. It's not the kind of thing one imagines happening."

"I did," Genaa said. "I didn't really expect it, of course. But I did imagine—"

But it was just then that the hangings of the inner doorway stirred, and then were pushed aside to reveal the figure of a large stately man dressed in a shuba of purest white.

"Greetings, Chosen Ones," he said, smiling. "I am D'ol Regle, master of novices and your guide and guardian during the next four years."

Raamo and Genaa hurried forward to touch D'ol Regle's hand and join him in the greeting.

"Come then, children," he said, when the familiar words were completed, "I am to present you to your new family."

The rest of the morning was, for Raamo, an exhilarating confusion, a surfeit of new and strange experiences and emotions. Following D'ol Regle, Raamo and Genaa were first led down a long hallway past many small chambers and then through a large archway where another Ol-zhaan—this one very youthful and wearing the short green tabard of a novice over his shuba—sat at watch. In response to D'ol Regle's nod, the novice released the door-net of heavy cord and allowed them to pass.

Inside this inner doorway, D'ol Regle halted. He waited until the heavy hangings and doornet were back in place before he spoke. He was a large man, his body wide and weighty under his flowing shuba, and his voice seemed weighty, too, slow and ponderous with wisdom and dignity.

"Stop, Chosen Ones," he said. "Pause here and reflect that with the drawing of these door hangings behind you, you have entered the temple itself. Past this point are sacred hallways. Look around you and Joy in what your eyes behold, but—" he paused dramatically, "remember, that you must not speak of what you see—or what you hear or do inside these walls, except among your fellow-Ol-zhaan. All things here are holy and therefore secret." For a moment he held Raamo and Genaa with his eyes before he turned away and proceeded down the hall, his full body rolling from side to side with the measured solemnity of his stride.

Greatly affected by D'ol Regle's imposing presence— even his size and shape seemed wondrously impressive— Raamo hurried after the stately figure, silent and full of wonder. He hardly noticed Genaa's elbow nudging him until she nudged again, much harder. When Raamo finally glanced at her, she rolled her eyes and smiled, as if to share a joke. Raamo smiled back uncertainly, tried to pense her meaning, failed, and then hurried on after D'ol Regle.

The hallway, wider here, was hung with beautiful tapestries, intricately embroidered with strange and unfamiliar scenes. Here and there in alcoves and niches, decorative objects sat on pedestals. Some of the objects seemed to be urns and bowls, but they were not fashioned from wood or gourd. Instead they were of a strange transparent material, clear and colorless, like water enchanted into solid form. On other pedestals were statues of human figures and of what seemed to be animals, but animals unlike any that Raamo had ever seen. These figures were, again, fashioned of materials that were entirely unfamiliar. Some were mottled gray and white, but of a cool hardness of surface, and others, reddish brown in color, gleamed with a hard brilliance that caught and reflected light as did the brightest feathers of certain birds. But when Genaa attempted to question D'ol Regle concerning the objects, he would only say that they were works of art and that their origin would be explained at the proper time and in the proper order.

They came, at last, to another large archway, and through it D'ol Regle led them into a large assembly hall. The hall was full of Ol-zhaan. Seated around an enormous table-board were more than forty men and women of all ages, who looked up at them as they entered. As the many pairs of searching eyes met Raamo's, he began again to feel the quivering pulsing agitation that had troubled him the day before. Only a few times in his life had he exchanged eye-touch with even one Ol-zhaan, and now to stand before so many filled him with disquieting sensations. Instinctively his eyes fell. Unable to raise his eyes, he tried instead to collect himself enough to center his Spirit-force in sending, so that the Ol-zhaan might pense his gratitude and devotion.

D'ol Regle was speaking, naming Raamo and Genaa, and then leading them around the table to greet each of the Ol-zhaan individually. Several he had seen before. He recognized D'ol Birta, a woman of middle age who came often to the Garden to counsel the teachers. A few others Raamo remembered seeing at public meetings and ceremonies. And at the head of the table sat D'ol Falla, the tiny, green-eyed ancient who had spoken to him at his counseling and whom he had seen in the place of honor at the rear of the Vine Procession.

Approaching D'ol Falla, Raamo raised his eyes with great effort and for only a moment he looked into the eyes of the old woman. They were large eyes, clear and deep and of an intensely brilliant shade of green. They seemed to Raamo to be full of ancient wisdom and at the same time strangely youthful; they stared into Raamo's with an intensity that was almost painful.

It seemed to Raamo that the faces of all the Ol-zhaan, whether strange or familiar, were alike in their glory and majesty. Wreathed in the glowing sheen of their shuba hoods, they seemed to be surrounded by a mysterious aura no less awesome than the cloud-spun wreaths of light that often glorified the brightest of Green-sky's moons.

When the rounds of greetings were over at last, Raamo and Genaa were taken to a smaller chamber where, alone again with D'ol Regle, they listened while he spoke at length, instructing and exhorting. They were told to continue to be silent about the choosing until the general assembly, except with their own families, and to mind-block carefully if they were in contact with children who might be young enough to pense and yet old enough to understand what it meant to be a Chosen. In the meantime they were to help their families prepare to move to new nid-places on the lowest level of Grandgrund. On the morning of the assembly, they were to return to the outer temple with their families, two hours before the time the assembly was to begin.

The instructions of D'ol Regle were given in voice-speaking, loudly and clearly, but they reached Raamo, through the haze of his excitement, as uncertainly as the weak sendings of a half-blocked mind. It was not until he and Genaa had been escorted to the inner gate, and D'ol Regle had left them, that Raamo realized just how little he had retained. His emotions, his response to the events of the morning, he remembered well—would always re-member. But the facts, the carefully detailed instructions, were blurred and unclear.

"Good-bye then, until the morning of the assembly," Genaa said, offering her palms for the ritual of parting.

And Raamo had to ask, "At what hour? At what hour did D'ol Regle say we were to be here?"

Genaa looked at him in surprise. "The tenth hour," she said. "Didn't you hear him?"

Raamo grimaced in embarrassment. "I heard him, but my mind was elsewhere. I do that often."

Genaa smiled, arching an eyebrow. "We are to wait in the large counseling chamber for the Ol-zhaan D'ol Fanta," she said. "Do you remember that?"

"Yes, I remember that," Raamo said. "Which one is she?"

Genaa shook her head. "She sat—" she paused, counting in her mind, "—fifth on the far side of the table. Of middle age—with a large chin."

Raamo stared. "Do you remember all their names?" he asked.

"I think so," Genaa said. "On the far side there was D'ol Druvo and D'ol Wassou and—"

Raamo shook his head admiringly. "I see now why

you were chosen," he said. "I remember only two or three and those because I had seen them before. My memory has never been—"

At that moment, while he was still speaking, Raamo was interrupted by a sending that spoke his name so strongly that he heard it clearly, although he was making no effort to pense. With no conscious effort, without even centering his Spirit-force, he found himself pensing someone who called his name. "Raamo," he heard. "Raamo D'ok. Look behind you."

Raamo turned quickly, but at first he saw nothing and no one. But then something stirred in a distant doorway where someone was standing in the shadows.

"Ah, it is true, then," the sending came again. "This time they have chosen well. And I, also, choose you. You are twice chosen, D'ol Raamo."

CHAPTER SIX

*T*he sun was high above the forest when Raamo set out from the grove of the Ol-zhaan, bound for his own nid-place in the upper midheights of Skygrund on the western edge of Orbora. The journey was not a long one or ordinarily very time-consuming. By climbing to the upper heights of Stargrund and from there beginning a glide that would take him through the heights of the two Gardengrunds and across the outskirts of Silkgrund, he could have reached his own home tree in a matter of minutes. Instead, he did not arrive until the sun was sinking beyond the far forest and the day was almost gone.

On leaving the temple grove, it had occurred to Raamo to climb high up into the upper branches of Stargrund and, among the narrow, swaying branches of the heights, to try to cross over the entire city until he reached the high branches of Skygrund. Up there, far from the press and bustle of the public branchpaths, with all the beauty of Orbora, the Temple City, spread out below him, he could be alone with his thoughts for as long as it pleased him.

He began his climb by way of Startrunk and, until the Vine ladders ended, he climbed very swiftly. But once among the myriad interwoven branches of the upper heights, his progress diminished to a leisurely exploration in the general direction of his home. He walked slowly along branches not much wider than a man's arm and scrambled to adjoining branches through networks of Wissenvine. Once or twice he slid down the smooth narrow trunk of a rooftree until, on a lower level, he was able to reach the branch of the next grund. And several times, when cozy moss-grown forks offered a secure resting place, he stopped awhile to think and dream. Swaying in the constant warm breezes of the high forest, he nibbled on tree mushrooms and thought of many things.

Swinging there, just below the rooffronds, as free and solitary as the high-flying rain dove, Raamo thought of his past life, his childhood, now so suddenly over. Looking back it seemed to have been a time of great happiness. A quiet time of careless freedom, of long hours spent with other boys and girls, climbing, gliding, and exploring in an endless playground of forest and sky. He remembered day-long explorations into the open forest far from the city, where he and his friends, supposedly searching for trencher beaks, had made other and more exciting discoveries. He remembered wild scrambles along untrodden branches after the small cuddly treebears, which, although easily tamed, were not often accepted by parents as nid-pets because of their big appetites and messy habits. He remembered the building of special meeting places in the branches of uninhabited grunds where groups of boys and girls who were close friends would meet to talk, to play games, and to practice the rituals of love and friendship that they had been taught since earliest infancy.

He remembered also, other times, when prodded by strange urgings, which left him feeling bewildered and guilty, he had, with a few daring friends, climbed down to within a few feet of the forest floor—although he knew well how dangerous and how disapproved such explorations were. But somehow, the strange tantalizing thrill had been too much to resist.

No Kindar was ever supposed to go below the lowest level of Grundtree branches, but by scrambling through tangled Wissenvines, or shinnying, sima fashion, down small rooftree trunks, it was possible to go much lower, without actually setting foot on the forest floor. Hanging there, perhaps a hundred feet below the safety of the great public branchways, perhaps even low enough to touch and be touched by the great feathery fronds of fern, or the smooth pale skin of a mushroom dome, the world of the forest floor was very near and incredibly strange and fascinating.

The air was warm and close and full of dark pungent smells, so different from the rainwashed breezes of the high forest. The earth itself, the rich dark soil of Greensky—a mystery to a tree-born Kindar—was visible in places where pathways wound in and out, worn bare of grasses by unimaginable paws or feet. From here and there beneath the undergrowth there came mysterious sounds, perhaps the skittering and chattering of small earth creatures—or perhaps something far more sinister. Was it not possible that the noises came from farther down, drifting up ventilation tunnels and out through the grillwork of Wissenvine? Or even more terrifying to contemplate, could the sounds be coming from very near—

perhaps from just below the nearest arch of fern-frond, where long clawed monsters—somehow released from their earthly prison—crouched tense and ready. Such thoughts were enough to send the bravest of guilty explorers scrambling for the safety of the great branches of the nearest grund.

Even now, when he was no longer a rebellious child daring to explore forbidden places, the thought of the forest floor and its mysteries was intriguing to Raamo. Forgetting for the moment the great responsibilities and honor that lay in his future, he let his mind drift over the possibility of descending once more to the lowest limits of safety. Rolling over onto his stomach, he looked down from his resting place, down and down, past branch and Vine, past branchpaths and nid-places, past the clustering buildings and hallways of the city, to where the earth lay—deep and dark and hidden, underlying everything— supporting, feeding, replenishing every spark of life in all of Green-sky. And yet harboring in its dark depths unthinkable evils.

"I'll go once more," Raamo thought. "Before I go to become an Ol-zhaan, I'll go down once more to the forest floor. Perhaps I'll even touch the earth with my bare hand." The very thought sent a convulsive shudder up the backs of his legs and along his backbone all the way to the base of his skull. A moment later he shook his head violently as cold disgust swept over him. How could he? How could he give way to such unworthy desires now, now when he had been granted such a high and sacred honor? What would the Ol-zhaan think of him if they knew? Surely they would reject him and choose someone more deserving to take his place as a Chosen.

Later in the day during the course of his long slow

journey home, Raamo stopped and rested again. This time he lay on his stomach on a springy branch and rocked with the breezes while his mind drifted, too, from place to place. He thought of his friends, girls and boys with whom he had attended the Garden for so many years. Very soon now they would be beginning their apprenticeships, and soon afterward they would be inducted into the appropriate guilds. After a year of successful apprenticeship, they would be free, if they wished, to move out of their family nid-places into one of the Youth Halls, where they would live a joyful carefree existence in the company of other young people.

The life of the Youth Halls was spoken of fondly and with nostalgia by older Kindar, who had long since chosen a permanent nid-mate and the more highly honored but less carefree existence of family life. Garden students looked forward to their Youth Hall years, and many of the songs and stories of the troubadours centered around the ever-changing romances of the Hall residents. It was a time of many and varied relationships, of testing and growing through close communion with many friends and fellow workers. Most Kindar lived for at least ten years in Youth Halls before they chose to form a family and move to private nid-places.

Family life was highly honored in Green-sky and seriously prepared for, and no one was eligible for the ritual of bonding until he or she was in his twenty-fourth year. But there came a time, for most Kindar, when the bustle of group activities and the ever-changing relationships of the Halls seemed less fulfilling than the richly rewarding Joys of family and children.

There were no children born in the Youth Halls. All

the residents were required to take part in weekly ceremonies in which Youth Wafers were distributed—large
flaky tablets that, when consumed regularly, produced
temporary sterility. Children were greatly loved in Green-
sky and admired for their natural gifts of Love and Spirit.
Nearly all Kindar wished to become parents, so a time
usually came when a permanent nid-mate was chosen, a
bonding ritual was performed, a new surname chosen,
and the new family moved into its own nid-place.

Such were the probabilities that Raamo's friends had
to look forward to; but his own probabilities were much
more uncertain and mysterious. It occurred to Raamo that
he did not even know if Ol-zhaan had nid-mates. It was
a question that had never before entered his mind. Somehow the Ol-zhaan had always seemed so far above and
beyond the life of ordinary mortals that he had never
connected them with anything so human and natural.

Suddenly Raamo found himself thinking of Genaa,
the other Chosen. It seemed obvious to Raamo that she
was, indeed, well chosen. Remembering the graceful
strength of her bearing and the startling brilliance of her
dark eyes, he could see that she had been set apart from
birth—a child born to high destiny.

Perhaps I, too, he thought, have in my features and
bearing the marks of grace and wisdom. Perhaps, if I
could have seen myself clearly, I would have guessed long
ago. It is strange though, that no one has ever told me of
it—that I have not even pensed that someone looking at
me was wondering at the significance of such great
beauty. Of course my mother did say that she had long
suspected that I—

He stopped then, laughing. "Paraso!" he said to himself, calling himself by the name of the proudest and

stupidest of birds. "All mothers have such suspicions. Doubtless our mother suspects that Pomma, too, is destined to great things. Such is the way with mothers."

The wonder of it returned then in a great wave, and Raamo floated on it, marveling. He marveled at his choosing, at the grandeur of the inner temple and at the beauty of the faces of the Ol-zhaan. And, remembering, he marveled, too, at the sending he had received as he was leaving the temple grounds.

It was not often that he was able to pense without eye-touch—without seeing the sender, or even knowing who it might be. But someone who hid behind the hangings of a far doorway had called in mind-touch and had said that he was well chosen. And twice chosen—by the speaker himself.

"Chosen for what? Who was the shadow in the doorway, and for what purpose has he chosen me?" Raamo asked himself, as he rocked on the high branches far above Orbora. The question returned again and again to his mind as he made his way home to his nid-place in the midheights of Skygrund. He thought of it often in the days that followed.

Time fled by. Raamo stayed close to his nid-place, avoiding contact with friends and classmates. Not that they would ask him directly concerning the results of his Second Counseling, since it was traditional to wait until the public assembly when, after the presentation of the Chosen, all thirteen-year-olds announced their new professions and were honored at banquets given by the guilds that they would soon join. But Raamo knew it would be difficult to keep his secret from friends with whom he had once played Five-Pense, and with whom he had often practiced rituals of close communion. So he stayed at home busying himself with the construction of carrying bags of woven tendril, which he then carefully packed with household goods, in preparation for the day when he and his family would move to their new nid-place on the lower level of Grandgrund. In the evenings, by the light of the honey lamps, the whole family worked together preparing a new shuba for Valdo, his old one being somewhat worn and shabby and unsuited for such an important occasion as the assembly at which it would be announced that his only son was a Chosen. While Raamo, along with Pomma and Valdo himself, stitched and restitched the seams of the wing-panels, Hearba decorated the front and hood with richly colored embroidery.

A plain man, ungiven to finery, Valdo had never before allowed himself the luxury of so fine a shuba, and even while they worked he spoke scoffingly of such frippery. But when the shuba was finished and he tried it on, running his roughened hands over the rich smoothness of the silk, he looked down admiringly at the gleaming threads stitched into intricate patterns across his chest.

"It makes me feel—different," he said. "Like a different person."

"You look as grand as Ruulba D'arsh, the City-master," Hearba said, and Valdo nodded in agreement.

"I might, at that," he said. "I wish I could see myself. Pomma, make me a gazing bowl."

When Pomma returned with a wide bowl lined with dark grundleaf, and full of clear water, Valdo stared into it at his own image for several minutes, with unmistakable satisfaction.

On the morning of the assembly, the whole family rose very early, and long before the appointed hour they left their nid-place and started on their way to the temple.

The night rains had not long been over. Gleaming droplets lined the edges of every leaf, and the reservoirs on the roofs of the nid-places they passed were still full to brimming. Their first glide took them through the branches of the first Gardengrund and well into the eastern branches of the second. There they landed and briefly climbed again, until their height was sufficient to enable a second glide to bring them to the lower level of Stargrund. The ladders of Startrunk, usually so heavily traveled, were almost deserted, for few people left their nidplaces so early on the morning of a Free-day, when all working places and even the Garden were closed and silent. In only a few minutes the D'ok family had reached the midheights and the beginning of the ramp that led to the temple.

Until that moment Raamo had followed behind his parents. Whether gliding or climbing he had waited, as always, with his sister while his parents led the way. But now, as the outer gate of the temple loomed above them, Valdo stepped aside and motioned for Raamo to precede him. And so with his family following close behind him, Raamo pushed aside the rich hangings and entered the temple of the Ol-zhaan.

As Raamo had expected, since they had arrived so early, the large counseling room was deserted. The D'ok family sat down to wait. They sat stiffly, saying little, avoiding even eye-touch in their efforts to hide their agitation. Now and then Hearba glanced at Raamo and smiled, and then quickly looked away, obviously afraid that he might pense the unpeacefulness of her mind. At last the hangings of the outer doorway stirred and Genaa D'anhk entered accompanied by a woman. The woman, as tall as Genaa and with a suggestion of the same dark brilliance, was clearly her mother. Approaching the D'ok family, the mother gave her name, Jorda D'anhk, and offered her palms in greeting. The greetings were scarcely over when a youthful novice entered and then drew back the hangings to permit the entry of a tall, firm-chinned woman of middle age, the Ol-zhaan D'ol Fanta.

"Greetings, Chosen Ones and honored families," she said. "You are awaited. May I ask you to accompany me."

The room to which they were led was a robing room where several Kindar men and women, attendants of the outer temple, awaited, bearing every kind of ornamenta-tion—rings and amulets and plumed headdresses as well as a vast array of shubas. The shubas were made of a rare and highly distinctive silk, whose gleaming fibers were produced by an unusually small variety of worm. The resulting cloth was reserved for the use of the Ol-zhaan and for the official robes of Kindar of the highest rank and honor.

As they entered the robing room, Genaa's mother and each member of Raamo's family was met by a group of dressers and led away. Raamo watched as his father, too, surrounded by a small mob of dressers, disappeared into one of the cubicles, waving his arms and protesting that the shuba he was wearing had been specially prepared for the occasion and was quite grand enough for him.

"Come, Chosen," D'ol Fanta said. "Your people will be well cared for, and you will see them later in the assembly hall."

It was indeed later, much later, when Raamo again saw his family. Clad in gleaming white shubas and crowned with wreaths of golden tree orchids, he and Genaa were led forth onto the high platform in the center of the great assembly hall of Orbora. There below them, on a lower level of the great platform, among the City-masters and Guild-leaders and the directors of the Garden and the Academy, were Valdo and Hearba and Pomma, their familiar faces subtly altered by the strains and tensions of the day. The opening ritual of the long and complicated ceremony had begun and, surrounded by Ol-zhaan and clutching a cermonial urn and symbol, Raamo joined in the singing of the Spirit Hymn. But as his mouth formed the words of the hymn, he found himself sending in mind-touch a greeting to his family.

"Thus do I pledge with sacred touch—our Peace and Joy as one shall grow." Looking down at their upturned faces, he sent the words fervently and with all the Spirit-force that he was able to call forth, unmindful for the moment that they could not pense and that the Ol-zhaan who stood around him surely could. It was not until he had completed the greeting to his family, that it occurred to Raamo that a greeting sent elsewhere during the sacred Spirit Hymn might be considered a sacrilege. For several minutes afterward he awaited a sending, reprimanding him for his offense, but none came, and the ceremony continued.

At last it was almost over. Each of the Ol-zhaan had taken part in leading the Kindar in songs and chants. The majestic D'ol Regle had spoken at length concerning the virtues and Spirit-gifts of the new Chosen, and the many signs that had shown the deliberating Ol-zhaan that these two were, indeed, the true Chosen, the Spirit-blessed and Guided, destined from birth for the temple and the leadership of Green-sky.

Overwhelmed by emotion, dazed and blinded by strange sensations, Raamo listened to the cheers and applause of the crowd until at last the cheering ended and a momentary silence fell in the huge hall. And in that moment he found himself pensing a sending that came from someone very near. There was no eye-touch as the sending came from behind him, but Raamo pensed the sent words clearly and distinctly.

"Do you like it, Twice-chosen?" the sending asked. "Are you learning to need the glory as you need air to breathe? It is meant that you should."

The sending stopped, and cautiously turning his head, Raamo searched the faces of the Ol-zhaan who stood behind him, and that of Genaa who stood at his side. The faces of the Ol-zhaan were alike in their noble calm, and Genaa's beautiful face glowed with the same dazzled emotion that Raamo had been feeling only a moment before.

"Who was sending?" Raamo sent. "Who was sending? Who was it that sent to me and called me Twice-chosen?" But there was no answer.

CHAPTER SEVEN

The Ceremony of the Choosing ended with a great procession down the central aisle of the assembly hall and out onto the public branch-ways of Orbora. Led by the Ol-zhaan and followed by hundreds of singing, shouting Kindar, Raamo and Genaa and their families were led out of the great hall and across the city center to their new nid-places on the third Northeast branchpath of Grandgrund.

Arriving before a new and spacious nid-place, the Ol-zhaan escorted the D'ok family onto the large open dooryard, and there, as two novice Ol-zhaan held back the door hangings, D'ol Regle asked Raamo to turn once more to the crowd and respond to its acclaim. With his family beside him, Raamo raised his hands in a gesture of gratitude and response as the shouts and cheers increased in intensity; they did not fade until at last he and his family were permitted to retire to the privacy of their new home. As the noise of the crowd dwindled, D'ol Regle spoke to them briefly concerning their new privileges and responsibilities; and then he, too, left and they were alone.

The room, the common room of their new nid-place, was enormous, and furnished in a manner far beyond the means of ordinary Kindar. In the place of the usual chairs and lounges fashioned of hardened tendril, this room contained many pieces carved from inlaid wood and covered with richly ornamented pillows. Since all woodwork was slowly and laboriously done by hand tools with cutting edges fashioned from trencher-beak, such furnishings were extremely rare and valuable. Walking slowly to the center of the room, the D'ok family stared uneasily at their magnificent surroundings.

A strange transformation had begun to come over them. Where, a moment before they had been glowing, shining, smiling—as alight with excitement and emotion as newly caught moonmoths—they were now suddenly limp and silent. Raamo moved slowly to the nearest chair and collapsed into it. He sat for many minutes, as unaware of his surroundings as if he were deep in sleep, as he listened to the thunderous reverberating echoes that filled his mind. Perhaps his eyes had rested on Pomma for a long time before he awakened to what he was seeing.

Curled into the corner of a carved panwood lounge, Pomma seemed reduced to the size of a sima, her pale face withered and wizened with exhaustion. Seated on opposite sides of the room, Hearba and Valdo, lost in their own minds, seemed not to have noticed. Crossing to the lounge, Raamo pulled Pomma into his lap, where she curled against his chest like a baby treebear. Softly he began to sing a Psalm of Peace, the one that likened the fall of the night rain to warm soft voices. The psalm had always been one of Pomma's favorites;

and as Raamo sang, she raised her head and smiled weakly.

Soon after, Valdo and Hearba joined in the singing, and as the moments passed, the recurring returning rhythms and the intricate close harmonies brought the singers back to at least a portion of their usual peacefulness and close communion.

"But we can't stay here tonight," Hearba said suddenly, when the psalm was over. "All our belongings are still in our old nid-place in Skygrund."

As if in answer, a woman appeared in the inner doorway. "I am Ciela," she said. "I am assigned as a helper in your nid-place. You will find, I think, that everything you need is here. You may, of course, send for any of your old possessions if you think you will have further need of them. But this nid-place has been provided for you with the best of everything. Food, clothing, furniture, tapestries—"

"Baya," Pomma cried suddenly. "I want Baya."

The woman, Ciela, smiled. "Baya, too, has been supplied," she said, and disappearing briefly, she returned with the whimpering sima, who immediately scampered to Pomma and, leaping into her arms, clung to her neck.

Smiling, Hearba offered her palms to the woman in greeting. "I thank you," she said, when the greeting was completed, "for your kindness in coming to help us find our way about in this huge nid-place on this long day, which has left us quite exhausted. But perhaps you should quickly show us where we are to eat and sleep, as the night rains will soon begin and you will be unable to reach your own nid-place."

"You do not understand," Ciela said. "My nid-place is here. I am assigned. You will find that with your special duties and responsibilities as the parents of a Chosen, you will have little time for such tasks as nid-weaving and food preparation."

"Valdo?" Hearba said questioningly, clearly asking him to intervene, and Raamo easily pensed her distress at the thought of sharing their nid-place with a stranger. But when Valdo responded by offering his thanks to Ciela, Hearba tried again. "We have always cared for our own—" she was saying when Ciela interrupted.

"You have never had the care of so large a nid-place," Ciela said, "nor the many responsibilities of a Chosen family. I think you will find that you need my help."

"Who is it that sends—" Hearba began haltingly, and then paused, troubled that the stranger might find her thoughtless and ungrateful.

"By whom was I assigned?" Ciela asked. "By the Ol-zhaan. There is a helper assigned by the Ol-zhaan to the family of every Chosen, as I have been assigned to you."

Hearba bowed her head to signify her acceptance of the wisdom of the Ol-zhaan, the holy leaders of Green-sky.

In the days that followed, Raamo remained with his family in the new nid-place. Just as before, his father and mother went daily to work as harvester and embroiderer, and Pomma returned to her classes at the Garden. But there were many differences.

The D'ok family members were now persons of honor, and as such they found many differences in old familiar situations and relationships. People with whom they had long worked and played—friends with whom they had, only a few weeks before, danced and sung in the grundhalls, beloved friends with whom, in their Youth Hall days, they had once daily practiced rituals of close communion, even those with whom, as infants, they had once played Five-Pense—all these now stepped aside to let them pass and even asked them for advice in important matters—as if they had suddenly become authorities on everything from the nesting habits of trencher birds to the best way to cure an infant of fits of tearfulness.

Relationships within the family changed also, at least for a time. But as the days went by, old habits overcame newly acquired attitudes of respect and reverence—and soon Raamo was scolded and instructed by his parents and teased by his sister very much as before. At times it was hard for them to remember that he was soon to be transformed into a being of holy wisdom and great power. There were times when Raamo, himself, was almost able to forget.

There were, however, many reminders. From time to time a messenger, usually one of the novice Ol-zhaan, would arrive to escort Raamo to the temple to take part in a ceremony or celebration, or to a guild or assembly hall where he was to be honored at a public gathering or banquet. At such times Raamo and Genaa proceeded along branchpaths in a small procession, led by a symbol-bearing novice and followed by small crowds of admiring Kindar. Gradually Raamo became accustomed to the crowds and began to expect and enjoy the shouts of praise and commendation. The gracious gesture of response and gratitude became easy, and almost as natural as a smile.

"Why do they cheer and shout for the Chosen only during their year of honor?" Raamo asked their novice guide one day while they were on their way to the temple.

They had just reached the midheights of Stargrund, and the cheering crowds had been left behind. The novice, a short, round-faced youth called D'ol Salaat, had, himself, been a Chosen only the year before. His glance was quick and narrow as Raamo went on, "I don't understand why there is no more cheering once the Chosen has become an Ol-zhaan."

"It is the custom," D'ol Salaat said. Although he had accompanied Raamo and Genaa several times, he had spoken to them seldom and always with great brevity.

"It is because we are still one of them," Genaa said. "We are still Kindar, and therefore not too holy to be cheered and shouted at. Besides fame and honor probably mean nothing to the Ol-zhaan, and cheering would only offend their dignity. Is that not so, D'ol Salaat?"

D'ol Salaat's stately stride continued for a few more paces before he nodded approvingly. "You are quite right, Chosen One," he said. "When one has been elevated and is truly an Ol-zhaan, one places little value on the praise of the Kindar. As a true Ol-zhaan, you will learn to lift your eyes to higher matters."

While D'ol Salaat's eyes were lifted expressively, Genaa rolled hers toward Raamo in a manner that was not entirely respectful to the young Ol-zhaan. But by the time D'ol Salaat's eyes had descended to her level, Genaa's were again wide and admiring.

"I am sure that one learns many things of great importance when one becomes a novice—and a true Ol-zhaan," Genaa said in a voice of unnatural sweetness. Raamo had begun to suspect that when Genaa sounded like an artless child, it was best to be wary. But apparently D'ol Salaat had no such suspicions. He smiled at Genaa, allowing a small crack in his shell of dignity.

"One does indeed," he said. Then a sigh escaped him. "When one is a novice," he said, "one learns—continually. There are classes and lessons and examinations from morning until night. When one is still a Chosen and being fed and honored all over Green-sky, one doesn't know how lucky—" He stopped suddenly. After glancing sharply at Raamo and Genaa, he turned away and once more assumed his stiffly formal manner. "We must hurry on," he said. "We are awaited in the chambers of D'ol Regle."

During the long days of their year of honor, Raamo and Genaa were often together. During the moments in the temple while they awaited the beginning of a ceremony or the arrival of an Ol-zhaan, they spoke together briefly, with frequent interruptions. But on the long journeys to the other cities of Green-sky, they sometimes walked together and it was at such times that Raamo came to learn many things about Genaa D'anhk. And the more he learned, the more certain he became that she was, indeed, a person of great ability and rare talents. There was, for instance, little doubt that she was possessed of mental powers far beyond that of ordinary Kindar.

It was not only that her memory was remarkable—she had apparently memorized quickly and almost without effort not only every song and chant but also every story and history that the Garden had been able to provide. To Raamo, whose memory had always been untrustworthy, this alone seemed a remarkable feat. But there was more. If Genaa's remarkable memory put everything she had ever seen and learned in the past forever at her command, she was in even more extraordinary control of the present. It seemed to Raamo that Genaa absorbed everything—people, events, ideas, essences—with amazing speed and clarity. Each was instantly absorbed and analyzed and judged. And nothing was safe from the cutting edge of Genaa's mind and the prick of her mocking humor. But while nothing escaped Genaa, she herself escaped everything. Nothing, no person or situation seemed to touch or trouble her. Or so Raamo thought until one day when the Procession of Honor was on its way to the city of Farvald.

This procession, to the smallest and most isolated of the seven cities, had taken several days and now, as they approached their destination, the small column moved very slowly. The entire distance had been covered on foot, as D'ol Regle would not permit gliding while in procession—not even in open forest. When the portly novicemaster had explained that gliding, as a means of progression, was lacking in the dignity and majesty so necessary to the occasion, Genaa had whispered to Raamo that D'ol Regle would probably like gliding better if he liked sweetened pan a little less.

"He'd need wing-panels as wide as a branchway," she said, grinning at Raamo, and Raamo couldn't resist grinning back. "So we all have to walk for five days when we could easily have made it in two."

Raamo and Genaa were walking together well to the rear of the straggling column of marchers, made up of D'ol Regle and five other Ol-zhaan, six Kindar porters, and the families of Raamo and Genaa. Later on, as they approached the city, the two Chosen would have to take their places near the head of the procession. But for the moment everyone was too exhausted to trouble themselves over their whereabouts.

"Are we nearly there?" Raamo asked. "Do these grunds look familiar to you?"

"Yes," Genaa said. "Within the hour we should be reaching the outskirts of the city." There was no hint of eagerness in her voice.

"Aren't you pleased to be returning to your birthplace after having been so long away?" Raamo asked. "Many among those who cheer for you here as Chosen will be old friends and classmates. Is that not so?"

Genaa nodded. "Yes," she said. "And the thought is somewhat pleasing, if that is your meaning. But Farvald is not my birthplace."

"Where were you born then?"

"In Orbora. My father was then Director of the Academy."

Raamo stared at Genaa in astonishment. He had never before heard her speak of her father, and it seemed very strange that one would not speak of a parent who had held a position of such high honor. The Academy of Orbora trained teachers for the Gardens as well as those others among the Kindar who were destined for professions of great honor and responsibility. The Director of the Academy ranked with the City-masters at the very top of Kindar society.

Genaa turned her face away from Raamo's gaze, but not before he had read there something quite different from her usual clear-eyed composure. Pensing quickly he found, as he had suspected, that her mind-blocking was not complete. In that brief moment he pensed that Genaa's father was dead and that his death had brought her bitter anguish.

They walked on in silence. Finding it impossible to express in voice-speech, Raamo sent his sharing of her sorrow to Genaa in mind-touch, although he knew that she was unable to pense.

At last in voice-speech Raamo said, "And it was after the death of your father then, that you and your mother went to live in Farvald?"

"No," Genaa said, and her voice was again emotionless. "My father was sent to Farvald as a teacher in the Garden there."

This was indeed strange. That a man who had been Director of the Academy should be given a position of so much less honor. Suddenly an explanation occurred to him, "Was he, then, already too ill to fulfill the duties of his high office?" he asked.

"My father was never ill," Genaa said. "He was taken by the Pash-shan."

Something moved in Raamo's chest like a cold hand. He had heard, on rare occasions, rumors that a person in Orbora or Ninegrund or Farvald had been lost to the Pash-shan. But usually the person lost was a small infant too young to wear a shuba, who had simply fallen to the forest floor. Never before had it been a person closely related to someone he knew—and a full-grown man. Glancing at Genaa, who walked on steadily beside him, her face unchanged except for a vein throbbing in her temple and a blurring of her brilliant eyes, Raamo's mind darkened with thoughts too terrible to accept.

He was walking near the edge of the branchpath, and he carefully kept his eyes from straying downward, lest Genaa, noticing, might allow her thoughts to follow his. But although he looked straight ahead, the eyes of his mind would not return from the dark tangle of undergrowth, the damp pungent earth, the yawning mouths of hidden tunnels and the quick quiet movement of sharp clawed hands. He walked on, lost in the darkness of his thoughts, until a joyful shout aroused him.

A welcoming procession of City-masters and singing Kindar from the city of Farvald were approaching along the branchpaths of the next grundtree.

CHAPTER EIGHT

*T**he journey to Farvald** was only one of six long journeys, one to each of the outlying cities of Green-sky. In each of these smaller cities, whether in lonely Farvald or busy bustling Grundbaum, the celebrations for the Chosen made up for whatever they lacked in lavishness and sophistication by their joyousness and enthusiasm. In each of these provincial cities, the entire local community of Ol-zhaan, usually around fifteen in number, took part in the welcoming procession and in all of the other ceremonies and banquets. And every Kindar in the entire area turned out along the public branchpaths to sing and dance and cheer.

They sang the same songs in all seven cities, songs praising the wisdom and beauty of the Chosen, but in the six smaller places Joy seemed more deep and real than it had in Orbora. Raamo took pleasure in that Joy, even though he suspected that Genaa was right when she said that it was largely because the inhabitants of the quiet provincial cities had few public entertainments and therefore welcomed any kind of diversion. But regardless of the reason for their delight, it was obviously great and real and Raamo shared in it. He liked, also, the long quiet journeys through the open forest, and he would have looked forward to each one had it not been for his sister, Pomma.

As the year passed, Raamo's fears for Pomma grew. Daily she seemed to be more thin and pale and her enormous bluegreen eyes seemed larger and larger in her tiny face. Raamo was sure that the long journeys and the excitement of strange surroundings and cheering crowds strained her meager store of strength. However, custom required that the families of the Chosen accompany them on the journeys of honor; and in such matters, custom was not to be questioned.

Hearba, Raamo knew, was troubled also. Valdo seemed not to have noticed the change in Pomma, or if he did, he made no mention of it to Raamo. Caught up as he was in the duties of his profession and the absorbing responsibilities that had become his as a public figure and person of high honor, Valdo was constantly occupied. Seeing his daughter but seldom, the change in her was, perhaps, less apparent to him. And Hearba had not told him that she had taken Pomma to a Ceremony of Healing, not once, but many times.

It was already the month of three moons, not more than twenty days before the Ceremony of Elevation that would make Raamo a true Ol-zhaan, when Hearba spoke to him of her hope and fear. Valdo had not yet returned home, and Pomma had gone early to her nid to rest for a time before the evening food-taking. Hearba's words were for Raamo's ears alone.

"I fear for her, Raamo," she said. "We were again to the Ceremony of Healing today, in the small assembly hall in Orchardgrund."

"You have taken her many times," Raamo said. "Do the ceremonies seem to help?"

"But little," Hearba said. "And even that little seems to be of brief duration. Twice some months ago, when the ceremony was led by a young Ol-zhaan with strange eyes, she seemed much better for a short time, but only a short time. She spends more and more time lying in her nid or on the balcony outside her chamber, and recently she has eaten almost nothing."

"But she ate a nutcake and some fruit this morning," Raamo said. "I noticed it particularly."

"Yes," Hearba said, "because you were at home. When you are away at a banquet or at the temple, she eats nothing at all."

"But very soon," Raamo said, "I will not be home at all. During the first year of my novitiate, I will not be permitted to visit the home of my parents. You know that this is so."

Hearba nodded. "I know," she said. "It troubles me greatly. When you are no longer here, I do not know if—" She stopped, her eyes averted. She was smiling now, but Raamo saw her hands shaking from the strain it took to produce the smile and the cheerful voice with which she continued. "But I should not be troubling you with such matters on the eve of your Elevation. She will soon begin to eat again, I am sure. And then, when you have become a true Ol-zhaan, with all the power and Spirit-force of the holy healers, then you will conduct a Ceremony of Healing for her, and surely she will be cured. Surely you will be able to heal your own sister even though—" Hearba stopped again, abruptly, her eyes shadowing with obvious mind-pain.

"Even though?" Raamo queried. "I will be able to heal her even though what, Mother?"

The last trace of Hearba's smile disappeared and, covering her face with her hands, she murmured, "—even though she is ill of the wasting." She looked up again quickly at Raamo, and he pensed her entreaty that he deny it was true, but he could only stare at her in horror. "Today, after the ceremony," she said, "the Ol-zhaan told me that her illness might be the wasting. He did not say for certain—only that it might be."

Raamo's mind recoiled in disbelief. The wasting was rare in Green-sky, although in recent years it had become more common, and more deadly. It was said that, even in the olden days, there were people who moved and ate as little as possible, became thin and silent, and drifted through life without will or purpose. But in the olden days the victims lived on into old age, thin and silent Berry-dreamers, who were often able to continue in their professions, and who troubled the minds of their families but little. In recent times, however, the wasting more often moved swiftly to the final dream of death.

Raamo leaped to his feet, shouting denials and protests in mind-speech, although there was no one there who could hear and understand. No one, at least, who could pense his words, although Hearba, sitting quietly with bowed head, undoubtedly sensed their meaning. Lifting his arms in a gesture of confusion, Raamo paced to the window of the common room and stood staring out into the soft green shadows of late afternoon. Bird song and the clean sweet scent of the blossoming honeyvine only increased the bitterness of his mind-pain that this should happen now, so soon after the wonder and Joy of his choosing. It was an evil trick, a treachery, like a sharp and deadly thorn lurking in the midst of inviting petals. Pain and sorrow shook and consumed the depths of his being, leaving an aching emptiness. And into that emptiness came a vision, a foretelling.

At first it seemed only an imaging, a mind-picture summoned up clear and bright, as children do when playing Five-Pense. He saw, at first, Pomma as she had been some months ago—delicate and dreamy even then, but with healthy color still pulsing in her cheeks and her bluegreen eyes alight with mischief or merriment. But that image faded rapidly, in spite of Raamo's efforts to hold it, and was replaced by an image so terrifying that he shook his head violently, trying to drive it away. But it remained, a shadowy half-seen figure lying, tiny and alone, on a tapestry-draped platform, while from the darkness around it came the sound of solemn chants and soft wailing.

But then the image changed, becoming at the same time brighter and yet more indistinct. As Raamo watched, the small figure on the platform stirred and then sat up, reaching out toward another figure that stood in the shadows at the foot of the platform. It was then that Raamo realized that what he was seeing was not of his own imaging and was not, in any way, subject to his control. Wonderingly he watched as the second figure moved forward, holding out hands that seemed to be as small as the hands of a child and as dark in hue as those of a deepbrown sima. And then Pomma, for he could see clearly now that it was she, touched the dark hand with both of hers and, rising to her feet, began to dance. She moved lightly and joyously, singing as she danced a favorite children's song about a naughty treebear.

When the vision faded, Raamo still stood at the window, lost in wonder. Foretelling, the art of seeing visions of events yet to happen, was one of the rarest of the Spirit-skills. According to the old histories, it had once been much more common, but in recent times it was almost unheard of, at least among the Kindar.

"But some say the Ol-zhaan still practice foretelling," Raamo thought. "And I am almost an Ol-zhaan. Perhaps—"

He turned suddenly and approaching Hearba he said, "Mother, I have just had a vision—a foretelling vision. In the vision I saw that Pomma will not die of the wasting. I saw that she will be very ill but that she will be healed."

He spoke firmly and with a show of confidence, and the change in Hearba's face showed plainly that she accepted and shared his confidence. Her lips trembled, the tense lines in her face softened, and her eyes shone with hope and relief. Tonight she would sleep as she had not slept for weeks.

But Raamo lay sleepless, troubling not only over Pomma's illness, but also over the false assurances he had given Hearba—false because he was in no way certain of the meaning of his vision, or even if it had been a true foretelling. He knew very little about foretelling—how it was done or in what manner the future was made known to the foreteller. It was quite possible that he had only been imaging and building beguiling dreams on hopes and wishes, as Berry-eaters did on too many Berries.

But if his vision was not a true one, there were, perhaps, other ways to make sure that the hope he had given Hearba was not deceitful. It was true, as Hearba had mentioned, that he, himself, would soon be an Ol-zhaan, and as an Ol-zhaan he would surely be taught the skill of healing. Of course, he would not be able to conduct a public Ceremony of Healing until the end of the three-year-long novitiate; yet surely he might be allowed to heal privately before that time. But if it should happen that his force for healing was as faulty as his memory, or if he learned too slowly—what then?

The next morning before the novice D'ol Salaat appeared at the doorway to escort him to the temple, Raamo spoke to his mother concerning the Ol-zhaan with the strange eyes, the one who had been able to improve Pomma's condition, at least temporarily.

"Last night you spoke of a young Ol-zhaan who twice conducted the Ceremony of Healing some months ago. Do you remember his name?"

He had thought it quite likely she would not, since she would not have used his true name in any way. She would simply have called him D'ol-zhaan, because it was considered disrespectful for a Kindar to address an Ol-zhaan by his true name in a public place. However, she answered Raamo's question with a quick nod of her head.

"His name is—" she paused, lowering her voice to a respectful whisper, "—D'ol Neric. And his eyes are round and dark and they dart around." Hearba made her own eyes flicker from place to place. "Like Baya when she is trying to catch moonmoths," she added and then blushed, fearing that such a remark about an Ol-zhaan would be considered improper.

"I know the one," Raamo said. "I've noticed him often in the temple and at celebrations, and he accompanied us on the journey to Farvald."

"Yes, yes, that is the one," Hearba said.

"But I have not seen him lately. I think he was sent to one of the smaller cities some months ago."

"It has been many months since he last conducted the ceremony," Hearba said. "I have watched for his return."

"I, too, will watch for him," Raamo said.

"Was he the one, in your foretelling, who healed Pomma?" Hearba asked.

"It was not clear," Raamo said uneasily. "In the fore-telling there was one who reached out to Pomma and healed her, but the healer was shrouded in a hooded shuba and stood in the shadows. But the thought came to me last night that until we are certain who it will be, it could do no harm to take Pomma again to the Ceremony of Healing led by the young Ol-zhaan of whom you spoke, since he seemed to have helped her somewhat in the past."

Once again Raamo was speaking deceitfully to his mother. He had, indeed, thought of what his mother had said concerning the young Ol-zhaan. But his thought had been that, even if the help given was only temporary, perhaps it would at least give them some time. Time for Raamo, himself, to learn the skill of healing—time for the Ol-zhaan to find a way to cure the wasting—time, at least, to hope.

So it was that Raamo's heart lifted when, only two days later, while crossing the temple courtyard, he came face to face with the Ol-zhaan D'ol Neric. Raamo had just entered the courtyard accompanied by the novice D'ol Salaat, and Genaa. They were on their way to the great Temple Hall where the Ceremony of Elevation would be performed in a few days' time. On this day D'ol Regle was to instruct them and test their knowledge of the rituals and responses that would play a part in the coming cere-mony. Fearful lest his memory should fail him and make him appear stupid in Genaa's eyes, Raamo had been si-

lently rehearsing the words of the responses as they made
their way across the great central platform, and he almost
failed to recognize the dark-eyed, sharp-featured face of
D'ol Neric.

Passing near them, D'ol Neric was several steps away
before Raamo, suddenly realizing whom he had seen,
whirled and hurried after him. But when D'ol Neric, hearing pursuing footsteps, turned and saw Raamo, he hastened away, striding so swiftly that Raamo would have
had to run to overtake him.

Stunned with surprise, Raamo stood staring after
him, mindlessly, until he realized that he was pensing a
sending that seemed to fade away as if with the increasing
distance of the sender.

"Raamo, go back," someone was sending. "We must
not be seen together, now or ever."

The sending trailed away into silence, and at the far
end of the central platform, D'ol Neric entered a doorway
and disappeared from view.

"Come, Chosen," D'ol Salaat was calling impatiently.
"We are already late for the meeting with D'ol Regle. What
are you doing?"

"I wanted to speak to D'ol Neric," Raamo said as he
rejoined Genaa and D'ol Salaat. "I wanted to—to greet
him—on his return—to Orbora."

Though his eyes were averted, Raamo knew his two
companions were looking at him strangely; but he was
too stunned to really care. "So it was he," he told himself.
"It was D'ol Neric who sent to me once before here on the
platform and again during the Ceremony of Choosing. It
was D'ol Neric who called me Twice-chosen."

CHAPTER NINE

In the days that followed, Raamo thought often and with great bewilderment of the strange actions of D'ol Neric, and of the even stranger sendings that must, surely, have come from him. However, with the Ceremony of Elevation approaching, and with the obvious worsening of Pomma's condition from day to day, there was much else to occupy his mind. Several times he caught a glimpse of D'ol Neric's sharp-edged face and lean figure in a crowd of Ol-zhaan, but he invariably moved away quickly if Raamo tried to approach him. When the day of the Ceremony of Elevation dawned, Raamo still had not succeeded in speaking to him. On that day, a day that would bring great honor and glory to Raamo, and should also have brought him great happiness, his mind was a shambles of conflicting thoughts and emotions.

He arose early, long before the procession of Ol-zhaan would arrive to escort him to the temple, and alone in soft gray light of early dawn he searched for Peace and calm, as he had searched a year earlier on the day of his Second Counseling. Sitting cross-legged on the balcony outside his nid-chamber, he strove to become one with the calm beauty of the forest. By song and chant and meditation he soothed the torment of his mind until, as the sunlight broke through the thinning clouds and sent its gleaming shafts through the rain-wet forest, the woman, Ciela, appeared in the doorway and summoned him to the morning food-taking.

The Ceremony of Elevation began with a grand procession led by many musicians and accompanied by troups of children wreathed in honey blossoms and carrying enormous plumes of paraso feathers. The columns of Ol-zhaan, rank on rank of stately white-robed figures, seemed endless. For this one ceremony of the year, every Ol-zhaan in Green-sky was present, even those who had to journey to Orbora from distant Paz or Farvald. And at the end of the procession, dressed for the first time in the pure white shubas of their holy calling, marched the new Ol-zhaan, D'ol Raamo and D'ol Genaa.

The ceremony itself, in the vast, dimly lit Temple Hall, passed swiftly. Raamo sang the words of the sacred songs, made the responses, and repeated the solemn vows that transformed him forever from carefree Kindar to holy Ol-zhaan—leader, counselor, healer, judge, and priest, one of a small number, less than 150, in whose hands lay the destiny of thousands of Kindar men, women, and children. At the climax of the ceremony, Raamo and Genaa, having completed their vows of commitment, were led before the seated ranks of Ol-zhaan. There, from her central seat of highest honor, D'ol Falla presented each with a wand of office. Then, in their first symbolic duty as Ol-zhaan, they each in turn led the assembly in the sacred Oath of the Spirit.

"Let us now swear—" Raamo chanted, and paused

while the crowd repeated the words after him, "—by our gratitude for this fair new land—that here beneath this green and gentle sky—no man shall lift his hand to any other—except to offer Love and Joy."

The familiar words, so often repeated as to become meaningless, seemed suddenly new and strange and frightening in their hidden depths. Raamo was frightened also by the thunderous echo of the crowd to the weak thin sound that was his own voice. It was a hidden fear, obscure and nameless, but so strong that when, a moment later, Raamo was lifted high above the crowd in the symbolic Elevation, he felt something within him recoil as if in terror.

"No," he found himself sending in mind-speech. "Do not look up to me. I am only Kindar. I am only Kindar like yourselves."

The shouting and singing continued. Doubtless, none among the Kindar were able to pense him, except perhaps for a few children who were too young to understand what they had heard. But as his fear subsided and the full realization of what he had done became clear to him, Raamo looked back furtively to the ranks of the Ol-zhaan. Surely some of them must have pensed his sending, and their faces would show their shock and horror. But as his eyes passed down the lines of white-robed figures, he read in their faces only solemn pride, calm repose, and, in one or two, what appeared to be a brief attack of drowsiness. But then, halfway down the back row, a pair of eyes met his, staring up at him with bright intensity from under a white hood. Thin lips smiled crookedly in a narrow face and, as the eyes bored into his, Raamo pensed a sending as clear and distinct as the clearest voice-speech.

"So Raamo," D'ol Neric was sending. "I did indeed choose wisely. They don't have you yet."

The great hall still echoed with songs and cheers. Sitting stiffly on the ceremonial throne, held high over the heads of the crowd by a dozen strong Kindar men, Raamo stared back over his shoulder, unable to tear his eyes away from D'ol Neric, or to understand his meaning.

"I don't understand," he sent at last. "What is it that you want of me, D'ol Neric?"

The smile sharpened. "What do I want of you?" D'ol Neric was sending. "I want you to meet me here, in the great hall tonight. Beneath the Spirit Altar. During the first fall of rain."

"Why?" Raamo sent, but no answer came. "I can't!" He sent the words with all the force of his being, centering every fiber of his body and Spirit into the sending.

"You can," the sending came again. "Come!" And then D'ol Neric lowered his eyes and sent no more.

When the ceremony was ended and all the Kindar had left the Temple Hall and the grove of the Ol-zhaan, Raamo and Genaa were given the green tabards that marked them as novices and taken to their new home. There in a cluster of chambers built around a large central hall, they would live during the three years of their novitiate. Surrounding the central hall, which was used by all as common room, dining hall and classroom, were many smaller chambers, several of which were assigned to the private use of each of the novices.

As soon as Raamo and Genaa entered the Novice Hall, D'ol Salaat presented himself and announced that it was his duty as second-year novice to make the newcomers welcome and acquaint them with their new surroundings. This he proceeded to do with great thoroughness and ver-

bosity, making it immediately clear that the silent reserve
that he had previously demonstrated had been the result
of something other than natural inclination. As he chat-
tered on and on about everything from the seating order
at food-taking, to the singular honor of his recent assignment as Orchard Protector, Genaa's responses became
more and more openly derisive. At last, D'ol Druva, who
was also in the second novitiate year, intervened and led
Genaa away, leaving Raamo alone with his relentlessly
informative host.

Staggering a little from exhaustion, Raamo followed
D'ol Salaat from chamber to chamber, until at last, to his
great relief, he was left alone in the chambers that had
been assigned for his use. Climbing into the large, freshly
woven nid, he collapsed gratefully, staring up at the
empty honey lamp and trying to force the swarming turmoil of his thoughts and emotions into some sort of an
orderly and meaningful whole. He had made little progress when, sometime later, he was summoned to the
central hall for the evening food-taking.

The food was good and plentiful, and the other
novices were friendly and curious. Genaa, too, seemed
to be in excellent spirits. Apparently untouched by the
stresses and strains of the long day, she joined in the
conversation at the table with poise and self-assurance,
laughing easily and often, and coolly refusing to be pa-
tronized by the still busily officious D'ol Salaat. But
Raamo, still feeling tired and spent, and increasingly troubled by the memory of D'ol Neric's eyes and his strange
command, hurriedly finished his meal and returned to his
own chambers.

Time passed, the green-tinged forest light softened
and grew dim. The air cooled and freshened and at last

the silence was broken by a soothing murmur. The first fall of the night rains had begun.

Raamo rose from his nid and went to the window. What should he do? What strange secret purposes lay behind D'ol Neric's weird behavior, and what part could he, Raamo, play in those purposes? In vain, he searched his memory for a custom, a tradition or a rule that might help him determine what the proper behavior would be in the situation in which he found himself. For many minutes he trembled on the edge of a decision, moving one moment toward the window and the next back to the safety of his nid. Several times he reminded himself that he was now an Ol-zhaan and therefore undoubtedly possessed of a new and superior ability to act with wisdom and good judgment. But when his decision was finally made, it was surprisingly true to his old familiar nature.

Since his faulty memory failed to remind him of a helpful rule or custom that would solve his dilemma, his ever-troubling curiosity took over and made the decision for him. He very much wanted to know what lay behind D'ol Neric's strange behavior. Quickly, before his resolution could waver, Raamo climbed out his window and launched himself into the rainy darkness.

Night gliding was dangerous, not only because of lack of visibility, but also because the almost constant night rains quickly soaked through silken shubas, making them uncomfortable and difficult to control. Under ordinary circumstances, anyone who was forced to venture out at night confined himself to walking and climbing. But there was nothing ordinary about any of the circumstances in which Raamo found himself, and a short terrifying drop into almost total darkness seemed, at the moment, only a natural part of a completely unnatural whole. Once airborne, however, Raamo was immediately panic-stricken, and when, a few seconds later, his flight ended abruptly in a tangle of Wissenvines, he vowed to climb down them until he reached a firm footing, if he had to go all the way to the forest floor. Fortunately, however, the tangled network of vines soon passed near a narrow grundbranch, which led down to one of the large connecting branch-paths of the temple grove. In a very short time Raamo arrived at the huge arching doorway of Temple Hall.

The empty hall, dimly lit by three small honey lamps, seemed to have grown immensely larger than it had been only a few hours before, when it had been filled with the pomp and splendor of the Ceremony of Elevation. Seemingly endless expanses stretched away into deep shadow and then on into caverns of darkness. Except for the muffled whisper of the rain, the silence was wide and soft. And yet there seemed to be in the silence a deep secret meaning, as if the huge recesses of the ancient hall were alive with memories that spoke to Raamo of things too mysterious and important to be captured in any language of tongue or mind.

Straining to hear and understand, Raamo stood silently for a long moment, before a furtive movement near the central altar caught his eye and brought him back to the present with a shattering jolt. In the darkness, the white shuba of D'ol Neric was dim and shadowy, but his sending was strong and clear.

"Raamo," the sending asked. "Is it you?"

"I have come, D'ol Neric," Raamo replied.

Moving slowly forward, he was soon close enough to see the strange eyes, round and dark and restless as a sima's but at the same time possessed of a force as piercing and irresistible as unfiltered sunlight.

"I have come," Raamo repeated, speaking now in voice speech. "But I don't know why. What is it that you want of me?"

Grasping Raamo's arm, D'ol Neric led him to a small cubicle behind the altar screen, apparently a storage place for robes used in the many ceremonies conducted in the Temple Hall. Draping a richly decorated robe over Raamo's wet shoulders, D'ol Neric motioned him toward a carved panwood settee. Seating himself at the other end, D'ol Neric busied himself for several seconds with the arrangement of the settee's cushions, positioning them carefully for his greater comfort, apparently unmindful of Raamo's bewildered stare. At last he looked up grinning.

"Come, friend," he said, "relax and make yourself comfortable. What I have to say to you will take some time in the telling." His smile faded and he added grimly, "—and there will be pain enough for you in the hearing without further paining your tired bones."

"Pain?" Raamo asked uneasily. He remembered suddenly that D'ol Neric had twice conducted the Ceremony of Healing when his sister was among the ailing. Fighting a desire to walk away without asking, without having to face the answer, Raamo forced himself to say, "You are speaking, then, of my sister? Did you call me here to tell me that she is ill of the wasting?"

For a long pain-filled moment Raamo was sure that the frown on D'ol Neric's face was caused by the need to be the bearer of such terrible news. But then he realized that he was pensing—and pensing not a reluctance to cause pain, but only surprise and bewilderment.

"I know nothing of your sister, Raamo," D'ol Neric said at last. "I did not know of her illness."

"But I was told that you twice sang the Psalm of

Healing for her at the public ceremony in Orbora," Raamo said. "Her name is Pomma D'ok, and she only in her eighth year and small even for her age."

"It could well be so," D'ol Neric said. "I have led Ceremonies of Healing in Orbora many times. But I seldom know or remember the names of the ailing. I am sorry, but I have no news of your sister."

Relief washed over Raamo, leaving him limp and mindless, so that the strange words that were next spoken echoed in his ear chambers for several seconds before his mind allowed them to enter.

"But it is, perhaps, true that I called you here to speak of the wasting," D'ol Neric was saying. "I called you here to speak to you of the wasting of all Green-sky."

CHAPTER TEN

*H*e insisted that Raamo call him simply, Neric, except, of course, in the hearing of others, as the respectful title D'ol was only another symptom of the illness that plagued the whole planet.

"They set themselves apart," he said, "in every way possible. They make themselves unknowable and unapproachable—so that the Kindar will not learn the truth about them."

"What truth?" Raamo asked.

"What truth!" Neric repeated, his voice rising almost to a shout. "A thousand truths. The truth, for instance, that the Spirit-skills are gone—dead! The fact that any Kindar, picked at random off any branchpath in Greensky, has as much ability at pensing or grunspreking as the most honored among the Ol-zhaan. Didn't you wonder how I dared to send you messages that would have placed me in great jeopardy had they been intercepted by my fellow Ol-zhaan?"

"But you are able to pense," Raamo said. "If pensing is dead among the Ol-zhaan, how is it—"

"I am the only one," Neric said. "One or two of the

ancients were once able, but they are no longer. And my skill is very slight. I can pense only what is sent, and then only if the sender is skillful and possessed of great Spirit-force. Until your coming, I had not pensed anyone clearly for several years, except children, of course."

"But why?" Raamo asked. "Why has this happened?"

"Perhaps there are many reasons, but there is one that is reason enough by itself. For many years, now, no one has been chosen who was suspected of having any skill at pensing. I, myself, would not have been chosen had they known of my slight skill."

"But why then—" Raamo began.

"Were you chosen? Because they are desperate. They have tried everything else. They knew, of course, of your abnormal skill at pensing—and there were many who opposed your choosing, but there was one—D'ol Falla herself—who felt that your Spirit-force must be used. I had not expected them to choose you. I had almost resigned myself to the inevitable, but when I heard that they had chosen the child Raamo D'ok who, according to his teachers, was still able to pense and kiniport and grunspreke at the age of thirteen years, I was given new hope. I decided that there might be a way to stop the evil that is spreading in Green-sky—if only I could reach you in time. And if only you would help me."

"But what evil?"

"I don't know exactly—or perhaps I should say—entirely. Not yet. That is why you and your talent for pensing is of such great importance—as a means of—" He smiled ruefully, shaking his head. "I can see how strange and senseless this must sound to you, and how disturbing. Let me start at the beginning—at the beginning for me, that is—and tell you my story. Then perhaps you will find it more understandable.

"I came to the temple as a novice only four years ago. It is, I suppose, in my nature to be somewhat suspicious and critical, but I began my days as an Ol-zhaan full of eagerness and enthusiasm, and also full of admiration and respect for the noble and holy company in which I found myself. The Year of Honor had accomplished its insidious purpose, for me, as well as for others."

"Purpose? What purpose?" Raamo asked.

"What purpose do you think? Have you never considered why the Chosen is subjected to a year of unrivaled glory and fame? What purpose the banquets, the assemblies, the processions of honor may serve?"

"I—I don't know," Raamo said. "I did not think to question. I supposed that it was—a tradition."

Neric nodded. "And, as Kindar, we are not prepared to question tradition. But there is a reason behind the tradition. The reason is that the Year of Honor is a trap. A beautiful trap, baited by a lure as irresistible to Kindar as is honey to a moonmoth—the lure of fame and honor and power. Thus a humble Kindar can be caught and fed on pride and power until he is as unable to live without them as a Berry-dreamer to live without his Berries. To do this takes time, and it must be accomplished *before* he becomes an Ol-zhaan and begins to learn their secrets.

"But to return to my own story. I was, as I have said, as well prepared as any when I became a holy Ol-zhaan. Perhaps even better prepared, since there were reasons why the honor and glory meant even more to me than to most Chosen. However, for some reason, I have always had a tendency to see all things skeptically, and it was not long before I began to see things here in the holy temple grove that troubled me greatly.

"I learned very early, of course, as you will also, of the death of the Spirit-skills; though the Kindar are still led to believe that every Ol-zhaan can pense every thought, kiniport twice their own weight, and, by the slightest exertion of Spirit-force, send a full-grown Wissenvine spiraling to the treetops.

"This deceitfulness toward the Kindar weighed heavily on my mind, and it also troubled me to learn that even as an Ol-zhaan I was not free to make use of my own intelligence. As a novice it is easy to accept the fact that one's life is controlled and directed by the novice-master, but you will learn that there are other masters, in every field of service and at every level of honor and importance. The chain of authority stretches unbroken to a select few, the Council of Elders, and even beyond to a group even more select and less well known, of whom I will speak shortly. And it is this small group who control not only the lives of the Kindar but the lives of all other Ol-zhaan as well.

"It troubled me also to learn of the many problems that are plaguing Green-sky, problems that are never mentioned to the Kindar, so that they know of them only through rumor and whispered conjecture. Such things as the increase of illness, the barrenness of bonded families, the increasing number of full-grown men and women who are yearly taken by the Pash-shan and, most troubling of all, the change in the appearance of the Wissenroot, which the Vine-priests seem unable to remedy. All these things, as you will soon learn, are discussed constantly in Ol-zhaan assemblies, as is the growing fear that the withering of the Root will finally allow the Pash-shan to escape into Green-sky."

The words of Neric had filled Raamo's mind with dark clouds of fear and confusion, but he managed to ask, "But why, if the death of the Spirit-skills are allowing these things to happen, did they choose those who have no such skills, as you say they have done for many years?"

"I *said*," Neric said, "they chose only those who could not *pense*. I am sure they would gladly have taken one who was skilled in healing or grunspreking—particularly in grunspreking—if that person could not pense. But such could not be found. Unfortunately, the skills of the Spirit are closely related, and it is not possible to pick and choose among them. So they were forced to avoid true healers and those who might have possessed the power to control and direct the growth of plant life, in order to avoid the pensers. For these might have, by their pensing, discovered secrets—secrets that are kept hidden not only from the Kindar but also from most of the Ol-zhaan. And of which I learned only by accident."

As he spoke, Neric leaned forward, lowering his voice to a whisper. "It was soon after my own Ceremony of Elevation. I happened to be hiding behind a fall of tapestry in a small assembly room in the far-heights of the grove—a strangely isolated chamber far above the commonly used halls and chambers. Why I was there is unimportant. I was exploring out of curiosity, when I heard voices, and not having permission to be in the chamber, I quickly stepped behind the tapestry. It was not long before I realized that to reveal myself would bring much more serious consequences than I had at first imagined.

"A number of people entered the room. From my hiding place I could see nothing and hear only a part of what was said. But I heard enough to determine that I was present at a meeting of a secret group of perhaps twelve or fourteen Ol-zhaan who were known to each other as the Geets-kel. The tapestry behind which I stood was very heavy, and the voices were kept cautiously low, but I heard them speak of a place called the Forgotten where something of great importance was kept hidden. I could not identify many of the voices, but there were two that I was certain of, and one or two more that I thought I recognized. It was undoubtedly the novice-master D'ol Regle who spoke loudly and at great length concerning the need to recruit two or three new members into their society—into the Geets-kel—and there was some argument about the qualifications of those who were being considered.

"They spoke also of those being considered as possible Chosen. It was then that I first heard your name mentioned—and your unusual talents in the skills of the Spirit. The voice of the ancient D'ol Falla was unmistakable—like the sound of dry rooffronds in a high wind—and it was she who spoke in your favor. There were protests—arguments—but she returned again and again to your name, and to the withering of the Root. But later when she spoke for you in a general assembly of all the Ol-zhaan, she did not mention the Root. She spoke only of the need to restore the Spirit-skills. But it seemed to be the Root, more than anything else, that concerned these Geets-kel—that, and the Pash-shan."

The Pash-shan. Only to hear the name spoken caused Raamo to shudder, as if someone had plucked his spine like a bowstring. "What did they say concerning the Pash-shan?" he asked.

"Enough to convince me that something is known

about them that has been kept from all except these few—the ones that call themselves the Geets-kel. Something of great importance. Something that might bring an end to life on Green-sky—at least as we know it. There was one whose voice I did not recognize who kept repeating, 'the end of life as we know it.' "

"But why?" Raamo could not keep the words from sounding like a moan. "Why would they hide such knowledge from the Kindar and even the other Ol-zhaan? Surely if the Pash-shan are escaping, it would be best if everyone were warned of it. Even if there was little that could be done."

"It would seem so," Neric agreed. "There appears to be no reasonable explanation. I have considered every possibility. It is possible, I suppose, that the Geets-kel know that the Pash-shan are, indeed, escaping, and that we are all, Ol-zhaan and Kindar alike, doomed. And since there is no remedy, they might feel it is best not to let us know. To allow us to remain carefree and happy as long as possible. However, I, myself, would not agree with such thinking. I would want to know the truth, no matter how terrible."

"And I, too," Raamo agreed.

"It has also occurred to me that the Geets-kel might be in league with the Pash-shan, or in some way under their control."

"Under their control? How could that be? The Pash-shan are beasts, monsters. How could they control the actions of Ol-zhaan?"

"They are beasts, perhaps," Neric said. "But their minds are not the minds of simple animals. We are taught that they are probably capable of Spirit-force greater, in some ways, than our own, though used only in the service of evil. Perhaps they have developed a skill similar to the ancient one of mesmerism, and by its use have made the Geets-kel into accomplices in their evil purposes. But then, again, I have thought—"

"No," Raamo said suddenly. "I can't—I wish to hear no more." He covered his face with his hands and leaned forward, his body bowed as if in pain.

For several seconds there was silence, and then Neric spoke again. "Forgive me, Raamo," he said. "I should have realized that it would be unwise to tell you so much so soon—and on this day when you were already exhausted. But I had waited so long for someone who might help penetrate the secret further. I was afraid to speak to you too soon, for fear that, knowing the truth, you would simply refuse to become an Ol-zhaan, and would therefore be of no use to me. And then, when I felt it was almost time, I was suddenly sent away to Grundbaum, and only allowed to return a few days ago. But I see now I should have waited a few days longer. I should have waited—even if the time left to us may not be long."

"The time left to us?" Raamo's voice shook with exhaustion and dispair. "The time left to do what? What is it that you expect of me? What can I do?"

"Ah." Neric moved closer to Raamo. "That is what we must discover first. By making use of your ability to pense and—"

"But I have already discovered that the Ol-zhaan mind-block very carefully," Raamo said. "And I cannot pense those who are mind-blocking."

"But surely if you watch and listen constantly there will be moments when someone is careless," Neric said. "And in the meantime it might be best if you pretended that your skill is less than it is. Or that you suddenly find it to be failing. If they believed that, they might be less careful in your presence."

Neric stood suddenly and pulled Raamo to his feet. "But come," he said. "We will speak again soon. But for now we must get you to your nid as soon as possible. You look like one far gone of the—" He broke off suddenly. "Did you say you have a sister who is ill of the wasting?"

But when Raamo tried to answer he found that his voice would not obey him. He stared at Neric helplessly, his lips trembling.

"In mind-speech then," Neric said, holding out his hands.

With the aid of palm-touch, Raamo found that he and Neric were able to pense each other with amazing speed and clarity. Like two infants who had attained the highest level in the game of Five-Pense, they sent and received quickly and easily, in distinct words and syllables. And in mind-speech Raamo explained to Neric about Pomma— how it was possible that she was wasting, and how she had twice received some comfort from healing cere-monies that Neric had conducted.

"I will do what I can for her," Neric said, "and I wish that I could promise more than that. I cannot say how much I wish it. When my field of service was assigned during my novitiate, it was decided that I should serve as a healer. Not because I had shown any particular force for healing, but only because it was necessary to choose someone and none among the younger Ol-zhaan seemed any better qualified. I did not want the assignment, for I felt I was deceiving the Kindar who came to the cere-monies believing that I was skilled in healing. But then I saw that I could be, at least, of some comfort, and at times when there was strong belief on the part of the ailing, there was, perhaps, some small degree of real healing. I tell you this because I would not deceive you when I tell you that I will seek your sister out and do what I can for her."

Raamo answered, "I thank you, Neric, and I will think carefully concerning all that you have told me tonight and—"

"And we will speak again very soon," Neric finished, and he led Raamo out of the great hall and, by a secret route that made use of steep narrow branchpaths and ladders of Wissenvine, to the roof of the hall of novices. From there Raamo was able to drop silently to his own balcony and slip unseen into his nid-chamber.

CHAPTER ELEVEN

*V*ery early in their novitiates, Raamo and
Genaa agreed that the novice D'ol Salaat was
a true paraso, given to vanity and self-
importance. But they also agreed that on one matter he
had spoken with great truth and accuracy. When he had
warned them that they should enjoy their year of honor
because the days of a novice were full of work and study,
he had, for once, spoken with good reason. This fact
became apparent almost immediately.

It was, in fact, the first morning after the Elevation
that Raamo, emerging sleepily from his nid-chamber, entered the common room to find the large-chinned D'ol
Birta waiting to begin his instruction. This first class,
which D'ol Birta explained was of the greatest importance
to the new novice, was called Form and Custom, and it
concerned matters of great urgency.

Yawning and heavy-eyed, Raamo and Genaa sat before D'ol Birta each morning thereafter, either in the common room of the novice hall or in D'ol Birta's private
chambers high in the temple grove, learning long lists of
rules and regulations. The rules concerned such things as

the proper manner of address and forms of contact permitted between Ol-zhaan and Kindar, as well as between Ol-zhaan and Ol-zhaan. Some of the knowledge imparted by D'ol Birta, such as the fact that relationships of Love and close communion were permitted between Ol-zhaan, but that bonding and parenthood were prohibited, was of sufficient interest to catch the attention of even the scarcely awakened. However, it seemed a poor time of day to require the memorization of long lists and charts concerning the ranks and titles of each Ol-zhaan and the authority vested in each position.

There were times, during the early days of his novitiate, when it seemed to Raamo that the life of a novice was very like that of a Kindar child during his years at the Garden. Many of the novice classes were quite similar to those taught in the Garden, at least in method and approach. As a Garden child learned the Forest Chant, by imitation and repetition, Raamo and Genaa learned how to conduct an endless number of ceremonies and celebrations—how to administer to the ailing, how to take part in a Vine procession, and how to conduct a public celebration of Peace or Joy. It was necessary, they were told, for all Ol-zhaan to be well versed in many rituals, even though they would eventually be assigned to the one area of service for which they seemed best suited. Thus it became necessary to again spend long hours in memorization, which Raamo found as difficult now as he had during his years at the Garden.

Not long after the beginning of their novitiates, Raamo and Genaa began to attend a class taught by the novice-master, D'ol Regle, which was, at times, quite different from anything they had encountered before. In spite of Raamo's problem with memorization, there were times when the words of D'ol Regle, emerging slowly from the deep recesses of his trunklike chest, implanted themselves in Raamo's mind as firmly as Wissenroot on the forest floor. And this great, if temporary, improvement in his memory was all the more strange in that it occurred in spite of, rather than because of, his firm intention.

"Within these walls," D'ol Regle announced on the first day of this class, "you will hear and understand and then think no more of what you have heard, holding it only in the dim depths of your memory."

And thus admonished, Raamo, who had forgotten many things with great ease, found it impossible to erase from his memory one syllable of the puzzling and disturbing words of the novice-master.

"It is the duty and the responsibility of every Olzhaan, to hear and understand the tragic story of the origins of our civilization, that they may more fully dedicate themselves to the holy purpose that underlies every institution in our social structure.

"Learn then, D'ol Genaa and D'ol Raamo, that the first settlement of Green-sky, the mythical flight revered in song and story, was indeed a flight. A desperate flight from a far distant planet, which had been totally destroyed by the terrible curse of war."

As Raamo and Genaa exchanged puzzled glances, D'ol Regle wrote the letters of the mysterious syllable on a grundleaf tablet and fastened it to the wall behind him. W A R—the letters were large and clearly printed but were without meaning to the novices until the master began to explain their terrible significance.

During the days that followed, many other words were posted on the wall behind D'ol Regle's chair. Words that were, at first, only meaningless sounds. Words like anger—hatred—murder—execute—punishment—violence. The explanation of these words was not only frightening to the young novices but also acutely embarrassing. Reared as they had been in a society where any show of unharmonious behavior was treated as a disgusting obscenity—where a squabble of two-year-olds over a toy was considered a disgraceful indication of defective training—and where in describing human emotions the strongest negative adjectives were words like "troubled" or "unjoyful"—in such a society, the frank definition of the meaning of a word like violence was enough to cause lowered eyes and painfully flushed cheeks.

Along with the strange new words—not new actually, as D'ol Regle carefully explained, but old and obsolete—the novices also learned many new facts concerning the beginnings of their civilization. They were told how, long ago on a distant planet, a group of learned holy men had managed to escape the destruction of their world. Foreseeing the holocaust, they had prepared for their escape and that of a large group of Kindar who had been entrusted to their care and instruction. The flight from the ravaged planet to Green-sky, Raamo and Genaa were surprised to learn, had taken several years.

In the beautiful history books of the Garden, the flight had been described but vaguely, and in the embroidered illustrations it was shown as a large group of people gliding through open space, apparently supported only by the wings of their shubas. However, the flight was actually made, D'ol Regle explained, by means of an enormous flying chamber constructed of materials called metals, which were unknown on Green-sky because of the Pash-shan. These materials, which were found beneath the surface of the land, were, of course, inaccessible in a country where such areas were in the control of monsters. For this reason metals existed in Green-sky only in relics of the flight—in the objects of art that lined the central hallway of the inner temple and in certain other ancient tools and artifacts that had been carefully preserved.

The metal flying chamber having arrived safely on a lush and beautiful planet, the group of holy men set about establishing a new society. Haunted, as they were, by the horrible fate of their beloved homeland, they, who were to become the first Ol-zhaan, dedicated themselves to the development of a civilization that would be free, not only of war, but also of all the evil seeds from which it had sprung.

Thus it was that these brilliant and learned men, by making use of their great knowledge of the human mind and of their mastery of the skills of the Spirit, were able to banish from the hearts and minds—even from the tongues—of their young charges, every semblance of violence. All the old institutions that had once given rise to hostile feelings were completely abandoned. In their place new institutions were developed in which all natural human instincts and drives were gratified in such a way that the pleasure of their gratification was closely associated with ritualized expressions of peaceful, joyful human communion. As a result, even the first generation in Green-sky had begun to demonstrate new heights of mind and Spirit.

"But what of the Pash-shan?" Genaa interrupted D'ol Regle's glowing description of the glorious success of the new society. "We are taught that in the days of the flight the Pash-shan were not yet imprisoned by the Root.

Weren't many of the Kindar lost to the Pash-shan in those early days?"

"In those early days," D'ol Regle said, "the Kindar were very few, and they lived high in the grundtops in chambers constructed for them from materials salvaged from the flying chamber. The Pash-shan, who lived far below on the forest floor, did not threaten them during those early years. It was only much later when the Pash-shan, growing strong in number, and jealous of the beauty of the Kindar civilization, became a great danger. And it was then that the great leader D'ol Wissen, famous in song and story, gathered those among the Ol-zhaan most gifted in the art of grunspreking and led them on the first Procession of the Holy Vine. There on the forest floor, amid constant danger from the Pash-shan, these few Ol-zhaan caused the already remarkable root system of a native vine to grow and spread until it covered the entire surface of the forest floor and at the same time to develop a magical strength, a coldly invulnerable force, which rendered it impervious to any attack made against it. And the evil forces of the Pash-shan were imprisoned in the dark depths of the earth. At that time, the Blessed Vine began also to produce Blossoms and Berries. Thus it was that the Vine brought not only protection from the Pash-shan but also the delicate beauty of the Blossom and the gentle comfort of the Berry to the people of Green-sky."

As D'ol Regle spoke, he had grown more and more grandly eloquent, as if he were addressing a large assembly of admiring Kindar. Genaa's quick glance at Raamo mocked the master's flowery speech, and her gesture of contrition mocked herself for having asked a question that invited such a grandiose and lengthy response.

"Yes, D'ol Regle," she said quickly when the Ol-zhaan

at last paused for breath. "We have heard the story of the first procession. I think it is in the fourth year at the Garden that one is required to commit it to memory. It was just that it had not occurred to me to wonder how long after the flight the Pash-shan were imprisoned."

"I have a question, also," Raamo said. "If the Kindar are protected from the evil emotions and deeds of our ancestors by their lack of knowledge of such things—by not even having the words to speak of such things—why must the Ol-zhaan remember? Would it not be better if we Ol-zhaan also could forget?"

"A thoughtful question, D'ol Raamo," the master said, "and one that has been debated by the Ol-zhaan in past years. The knowledge of our tragic past is, indeed, a burden. But it has been the judgment of our fellow Ol-zhaan that if the memory of violence was completely erased from our civilization, there would be none to guard against its return. Do you remember the chant In Praise of Good Memory?"

Raamo blushed. The chant had not been one of his favorites.

"I think I do," he said. "At least most of it."

"You recall then the line that says 'forgotten errors are soon repeated'? The words are true, and not only for children, but for civilizations as well. Therefore it has been decided that we, as Ol-zhaan, must bear the burden of memory, so that the tragic errors of our ancestors will never be repeated. Are you unwilling, D'ol Raamo, to bear such a burden?"

"No, no," Raamo said quickly. "I didn't mean that I was unwilling. It was just that I wondered about—" He paused and then finished lamely, "It was only that I wondered."

Raamo had always been tempted to spend too many hours on fruitless thought-taking, and now that he was an Ol-zhaan he did not seem to have conquered the tendency. As the voice of D'ol Regle rolled on, Raamo quite often found himself wondering about many things.

In particular, of course, he wondered about the terrible things that Neric had spoken of in the Temple Hall. About the Geets-kel and their fearful secret; about the fact that D'ol Regle himself was of their number; and about the possible connection between the Geets-kel and the Pash-shan. He wondered, too, of course, if what Neric had said was really true. As it happened, there had been no chance to talk further since Neric had again been sent away.

Only two days after their meeting in the temple, Neric had waylaid Raamo on a branchpath near the novice hall and told him briefly that he was being sent with a message to Farvald. He would not be gone long this time he said, no more than a dozen days, and in the meantime Raamo was to keep his eyes open. There had been no time to say more.

As the days passed, D'ol Regle eventually reached a period in the history of Green-sky that was much more familiar and much less shocking to his two students. The glorious early years on the new planet had been the subject of many of the songs and stories learned in the Gardens, and here, for the most part, D'ol Regle's telling differed but little from the traditional account. Raamo and Genaa heard, once more, in great detail, of the struggle to find food before the development of the huge orchards, of how the people had lived for years on little besides birds' eggs and tree mushrooms. But with the growth of the Spirit-skills and the art of grundspreking, the grunds and rooftrees were caused to die away in large areas, leaving open ground where carefully guided mutations of saplings brought from the old planet were then planted. These saplings adapted well to the rich soil of Green-sky, increased in productivity and, due to the light gravity, increased greatly in size. Soon food supplies were no longer a problem on the new planet.

D'ol Regle spoke also of the growth in the ability to pense, during those early days, when people of all ages were able to communicate beyond speech easily and fully. There were, of course, even then, differences between individuals in their ability to use the skills of the Spirit. There were those who could pense only with the aid of eye- and palm-touch; but there were also many who could pense anyone who was not blocking—and in those days mind-blocking was very rare. And since it was impossible to lie or dissemble in mind-touch, it was also a time of great honesty and openness in all relationships and in all situations.

The ability to kiniport was also almost universal, and teams of kiniporters, working in unison, could lift large logs and branches from one grund-level to another with little difficulty. Among the Ol-zhaan, Spirit-healers and mesmerizers were quite common, and they were able to cure nearly every ailment of mind and body. And Peace and Love and Joy had abounded throughout the land.

"But why is it no longer so?" Raamo asked. "What is causing the death of the Spirit-skills?"

"It is the Pash-shan. The Pash-shan are to blame."

Raamo had directed his question to D'ol Regle, but it had been Genaa's voice that had answered—Genaa's voice, but greatly altered in tone and pitch. Turning to look at her, Raamo saw that her face was tight with emotion.

"You are right, D'ol Genaa," D'ol Regle answered. "We do not know just how it is accomplished, but undoubtedly the evil Spirit-force of the Pash-shan rises up from their dungeons and somehow blocks the Spirit-force of Kindar and Ol-zhaan alike. We have known for many years that this was so, but we have not yet found a way to prevent it."

"Some say there are many evils caused by the heat-clouds that rise up from the mouths of the Pash-shan's tunnels," Raamo said. "I have heard that the wasting is caused by breathing air that has been made poisonous by the cloud columns of the monsters. Is this true, D'ol Regle?"

"It may be," the master said. "There is much concerning the Pash-shan that is uncertain. But it is sure that there have been many changes in Green-sky since the glorious early days, of which we have most recently been speaking. And it is of these changes that I must speak to you now."

D'ol Regle spoke with sad solemnity, and Raamo and Genaa found his words disturbing, although much of what he told them they had heard before as whispered rumors. But coming from the mouth of one of the oldest and most respected of the Ol-zhaan, the rumors became solid realities, and infinitely more frightening.

It was indeed true, D'ol Regle said, that the Spirit-skills seemed to be fading. With few exceptions, pensing had disappeared except among the very young. And while the Ol-zhaan, of course, still managed to retain much more Spirit-force than did the Kindar, it had waned there, too, to some extent.

D'ol Regle leaned forward confidingly. "It has been many years," he said, smiling benignly at Raamo, "since we have been joined by a novice with the Spirit-force of our young D'ol Raamo."

Perhaps it was because he was speaking with such a show of open frankness, that, for a fleeting instant, the novice-master's blocking was incomplete. He spoke approvingly of Raamo's skill, but even as he spoke, Raamo pensed, behind the smiling words, a deep distrust and anxiety.

Until that instant Raamo had made no firm decision concerning Neric and his strange revelations. He had tried to convince himself that Neric had been wrong—and at times he had almost succeeded. He had decided only one thing firmly, and that was that he would do nothing until Neric returned and they had spoken further. But now suddenly, listening to the smiling words of D'ol Regle, and pensing beneath them a coldness that spoke of fear or worse, Raamo found himself saying quickly, "But I have but little skill, D'ol Regle. And what I have had seems to be fading. I am no longer able to pense anything except that which is purposefully sent."

He spoke hastily, lowering his eyes before the surprised stares of not only D'ol Regle, but Genaa, also.

"Indeed?" D'ol Regle questioned. "I had heard that you were able—that your skill was greater?" He paused thoughtfully, and Raamo felt he detected a measure of relief behind the outward show of disappointment. But if D'ol Regle's response to Raamo's lie was devious, Genaa's was frank enough. Although she had no skill at pensing, Raamo found her sending was quite clear and distinct.

"You're lying, Raamo," he pensed. "Why are you lying?"

Under the eyes of the novice-master, Raamo could only acknowledge Genaa's sending with a glance and a nod, and Genaa stared back demandingly. Apparently unaware of the exchange between his students, D'ol Regle had returned to his accounting of the troubles besetting Green-sky. Kiniporting, he was saying, once a useful as well as an entertaining Spirit-skill, had almost entirely disappeared, and the much more important and crucial art of healing was even more completely lost. Illness, and in particular the distressing disease known as the wasting, was increasing, and every year fewer healthy babies were being born. But most troubling of all was the matter of the Blessed Root.

As D'ol Regle spoke, his full firm voice faltered uncertainly. "There is no doubt," he said, "that the Root is withering. In many places it has been observed that small offshoots have died completely, and in large sections the surface appears to be cracked and rough. There have been many processions, many attempts to control the condition, but to no avail. If a way cannot be found to bring the Root back to its full strength and invincibility, the Pash-shan may soon be free to roam at will in Green-sky."

"There are rumors that some have already escaped," Genaa said. "Are these rumors true?"

"Not to our knowing," D'ol Regle said. "We have not yet found a flaw in the grill of Root large enough to permit the passage of any creature larger than a very small child. But if the withering continues—"

"Then it is not possible for a Kindar, a grown man, to have been taken alive by the Pash-shan?" Genaa interrupted.

"Not alive," D'ol Regle said. "It is thought that when a grown Kindar is taken by the Pash-shan they are—" He paused suddenly, and it occurred to Raamo that the novice-master had only that instant recalled the story of

Genaa's father. As he faltered, obviously uncertain of how best to proceed, Genaa spoke again, her voice harsh and bitter. "They are *killed*," she said. "*Killed*. The word is, indeed, a useful one—just as it was to our ancestors. They are killed and cut to pieces by the sharp claws of the Pash-shan—and some say they are eaten."

As Genaa spoke, her voice rose in pitch and intensity, her whole body trembled, and at last she jumped to her feet and hurried from the chamber.

"May I be permitted to leave, also?" Raamo asked. "I would like to speak to D'ol Genaa."

The novice-master frowned. "Go," he said, "and tell D'ol Genaa that the Ol-zhaan do not allow their reason to be swayed by emotions. Tell her, also, that this discussion will be continued tomorrow."

Hurrying from the class chamber, Raamo found Genaa only a short distance away. She was standing near the edge of the branchpath with her head bent and her shoulders pulled forward. But when Raamo called to her, she turned quickly, smiling her mocking smile. Except for the liquid film that blurred the brilliance of her dark eyes, she seemed to have completely conquered her agitation. Before Raamo could find words for what he wanted to say, she began to speak.

"There you are," she said. "I was waiting for you. I want to know why you lied to old Regle about pensing. I know you can pense people who aren't sending because you've done it to me. Why did you lie about it?"

But at that moment a familiar figure appeared on the branchpath below them, striding swiftly in their direction. He passed by without pausing, with only a brief nod in their direction; but Genaa's eyes narrowed sharply as she noticed D'ol Neric's glance meet Raamo's and the sudden change that came over Raamo's face. She had seen him look that way before—his glance stilled and focused—his face radiant with Spirit-force.

D'ol Neric disappeared from view in the direction of the great hall, and Raamo turned hastily to Genaa and said, "We will speak of this soon, but for now I must go quickly. I have an appointment that must be kept."

CHAPTER TWELVE

*F**ollowing Neric at a distance,* Raamo watched him turn aside on a narrow branchpath and disappear from view. After waiting a few minutes, Raamo took the same branchpath and, climbing steeply, he came soon to a thick curtain of Wissenvine. As he approached the Vine, its leaves trembled and parted, revealing Neric's face.

"Come," he whispered. "This way."

On the other side of the Wissenvine curtain, a network of small branches formed a secluded hideaway. As Raamo squeezed past into the enclosure, Neric continued to peer out.

"What are you looking for?" Raamo asked.

"Did she follow you?" Neric asked.

"Follow me? Do you mean Genaa? Why should she follow me?"

Neric shrugged. "It occurred to me that she might. Out of curiosity, if nothing else. She is the kind that must know everything. It seemed to me that she was aware of something passing between us just now. Are you certain she cannot pense?"

Raamo smiled. "I've just discovered that she can send rather strongly when she wants to," he said. "But I'm quite certain she is not able to pense."

Neric frowned and once more peered out, carefully scanning the path by which they had come. At last, evidently satisfied that no one was approaching, he settled himself comfortably on a moss-covered branch.

"Well," he said, his dark eyes blinking rapidly as they searched Raamo's face, "what have you learned? What has happened while I was away?"

"What have I learned?" Raamo repeated, smiling. "A great deal more than I could tell you quickly. I have been in classes almost every waking moment since I last saw you and I have learned—"

"That's not what I meant," Neric interrupted impatiently. "I mean have you learned anything concerning the Geets-kel? Have you pensed anything, observed anything—" He broke off suddenly, staring at Raamo. Then he nodded sharply. "I see," he said. "I move too fast. I had taken it for granted that you were with me, that you would work with me against the Geets-kel. And I see now that you are uncertain. Am I not right, Raamo?"

Raamo nodded. "I have thought about what you told me in the Temple Hall, and I am certain that, if there is a Geets-kel and if they do know something concerning a danger to all Green-sky, they should be exposed, and their secret with them. But I have not been certain that these things are true."

In answer Neric held out his hands, and with palms and eye-touch made his sending as clear as voice-speech. "I have told you nothing that is untrue." And then in voice-speech he said, "Do you believe me now? You know that I could not lie in mind-touch."

"I know now that you were not lying," Raamo said. "But I was quite certain of that before. But for a time I did try to convince myself that you were mistaken. That you perhaps misunderstood what you overheard in the counsel room, and that it was your nature to make great issues out of matters of less than great importance." He smiled ruefully. "I tried not to believe you, but I found that your words had made me wonder about many things. And then, today—"

"Today?" Neric prompted eagerly.

"Today, in the history class, D'ol Regle spoke with approval of my Spirit-skills, but his blocking was not complete, and I pensed that, in truth, he had not wanted me to be a Chosen, and that he was, for some reason almost—" Raamo paused, shaking his head unbelievingly, "—almost afraid—of *me*."

"You see," Neric cried excitedly. "I knew it. I knew if only I could get your help that we would be able to discover the truth." He reached out and grasping Raamo's shoulders he said, "You are with me, then, Raamo? We will work together to discover the secret of the Geets-kel?"

Raamo sighed. "Yes," he said. "I will work with you until we find out the truth concerning the Geets-kel and the Pash-shan. I see now that I must."

Neric's round eyes gleamed, and his white teeth flashed in an excited grin. He gave Raamo's shoulders two quick shakes as he said, "Good! Good!" Then, moving with his usual jerky quickness, he rearranged himself on his moss-covered perch. "Now then," he said when he had his long angular body settled to his satisfaction with his legs folded under him, "we must begin to make our plans. With whom will you be studying in the days ahead?"

"With D'ol Regle, of course," Raamo said. "I believe the history class is to continue for some time. But I will also soon begin a special study of grunspreking and the rituals of the Vine with D'ol Falla."

"Aha," Neric said. "Does your fellow novice, D'ol Genaa, accompany you in this study?"

"No," Raamo said. "She is to go, instead, to D'ol Wassou for further study on the conducting of courts of judgment."

"Just as I thought," Neric said. "This means that your assignment to a field of service has already been decided upon. You are to be a Vine Priest, and your sharp-witted fellow novice is to be trained to pronounce judgments in the Kindar Courts. It is as I expected."

"No," Raamo said. "It can't be. Only a few days ago we were asked to state the service for which we felt we were best suited, and it was Genaa who asked to be assigned as a Vine Priest, not I. I asked that I be allowed to serve as a healer."

Neric's bitter smile was becoming very familiar to Raamo. "And you believed that you were to be given your choice? Have you not yet learned that there is little choosing done on our beloved planet, except by a very few? You were destined from the very beginning to minister to the ailing Root. Remember you would never have been chosen had it not been for the desperate need to find someone whose Spirit-force might be strong enough to guide the Wissenroot back to its former state. You will begin your study with D'ol Falla soon, and in a short time, perhaps next year, you will take your place as one of the nine who, in holy procession, descend almost daily to the forest floor."

Only a quick clenching of his teeth prevented Raamo

from making an audible gasp. Daily—to the forest floor! Fear and revulsion swarmed over him in a strange entanglement with other emotions that felt almost like exhilaration and anticipation.

Neric was watching him curiously. "Have you never thought of being a Priest of the Vine?" he asked. "Of visiting the forest floor?"

"Not really," Raamo said. "At least I had not really considered that I might someday be visiting the forest floor in a procession of Ol-zhaan, since I truly expected to serve as a healer. But as a child I sometimes climbed down nearly to the floor, and at such times I felt, somehow, that I was drawn there almost against my will—that I was somehow destined, or doomed perhaps, to walk there."

"I, too," Neric said. "How strange that we should both have felt such an attraction—such an irresistible curiosity. Perhaps—" Stopping in midsentence, he seemed to fall into deep thought.

Raamo, too, was silent, pursuing an idea that had just occurred to him. "Neric," he said at last. "I've been thinking—Genaa has, I know, a deep commitment to finding out more about the Pash-shan, and she is gifted in many ways that would be of great use to us. I wonder if it would not be wise for us to speak to her of these matters. I feel sure that she would feel as we do and that she could be of great use—" He broke off, noticing that Neric was staring at him in disbelief.

"You would tell that one?" Neric said. "You would put our lives into the hands of that daughter of privilege and birth-honor? You make me doubt my judgment of your wisdom."

Neric was leaning forward so far in his agitation that he suddenly lost his balance, and for a moment he struggled, flailing his long thin arms, in his effort to keep from pitching forward. When he had regained his equilibrium, he went on. "Your Genaa," he said, "is a natural Geets-kel. She will surely be asked to join their exclusive society. Remember I spoke of overhearing the discussion concerning the qualifications for new members? They spoke of ambition and superior intelligence and the consciousness of being set apart for a high destiny. In other words, they are looking for pride and arrogance and contempt for those who are less fortunate and less gifted. Your beautiful proud Genaa is exactly what they are seeking, Raamo."

Raamo stared at Neric in amazement. "I feel that you are judging Genaa unfairly," he said. "I feel certain that if you came to know her better—"

"And I feel certain," Neric interrupted shrilly, "that her beauty has swayed your judgment."

"Perhaps," Raamo said. "But something that concerns your childhood is swaying yours." He smiled apologetically. "You were not blocking and I—"

For a moment Neric glared at him, and then, rocking backward, he burst into laughter. "And you pensed me," he said. "And truly. You must know, then, Raamo, that my childhood does still sway me at times. My parents, both of them, were among the wasted. Not the kind of wasting we know now, which is sometimes swift and final, but the kind that made them into constant Berrydreamers, unfit for any kind of useful work. We lived in a makeshift nid-place, high up in the twigs of Orchardgrund, and ate and wore only what was provided for us by the charity of the guilds to which my parents had once belonged. They were outcasts—we were outcasts—and I blamed them and whatever it was that had made them what they were. I both loved and despised them. They died during my thirteenth year, and substitute parents were assigned me during my Year of Honor. But as you have truly pensed, I have not forgotten them—or my unfortunate childhood. It seems I am still harboring some of the resentment I had then for those who seemed more fortunate than I."

Neric laughed again, so freely that Raamo found himself laughing, too. At last, sobering, Raamo said, "I will speak no more of Genaa, at least for now. Perhaps we both need to look more carefully into our judgment of her before we consider this matter further."

Neric nodded, wiping his eyes. Then, his eyes blinking rapidly and his face twitching with the intensity of his feelings, he was suddenly deadly serious. "Have you heard news of your sister?" he asked. "I would have visited her long ago, had I not been sent so suddenly to Farvald."

"I have had many messages," Raamo said. "My mother hires a message bearer almost daily. But she says only that Pomma is much the same. I fear that, knowing I am unable to visit them or do anything to help, she is only trying to spare me mind-pain."

Neric nodded. "I will go tomorrow," he said, "and see for myself. And I will do what I can for her."

"I thank you," Raamo said.

"Do not thank me," Neric said. "I will be unable to do anything that is really helpful, except to bring you a true report on her condition. That much I will do early tomorrow morning. But as for now, let us continue with our planning. I was thinking, before we were sidetracked by our discussion of the beautiful Genaa, that we must concentrate our attention on the Pash-shan. I am sure that the key to the secret lies with the Pash-shan and their relationship to the Geets-kel. We must watch and listen for any mention, any unblocked thought, concerning the Pash-shan, and we must also investigate everything that shows evidence of their influence in Green-sky. Do you agree?"

Raamo nodded. "I think," he said, "that the withering of the Root is truly troubling to D'ol Regle. When he spoke to us of the evil influences of the Pash-shan in Green-sky, I felt—well, he was blocking of course, and I could not truly pense him—but I felt an edge of difference between the inward and outward meaning of his words. Until he began to speak of the Root. Then his troubling was true and deep."

"Ah," Neric said. "That is of interest. I wish that we could see the Root for ourselves. I wish you were further along in your novitiate and were soon to accompany the processions. But that will not be for at least a year."

"Then let us be our own procession. Let *us* go down to the forest floor." It was not until he was in the midst of speaking, that Raamo realized what he was saying. But even as a tremor of shocked surprise at his own audacity shook him, he was overwhelmed by a rush of other emotions. Fear and dread mingled in wild confusion with a strange feeling of relief, as if a voice, rising from the dark depths of his soul, was saying, "At last! At last!"

CHAPTER THIRTEEN

When Raamo proposed that he and Neric go together to the forest floor, Neric seemed, for a moment, to be stunned by the very thought. But only for a moment. Then excitement flared in his eyes like a sudden sunrise.

"Of course," he said. "Of course. I don't see why I hadn't thought of it before—except that we are so carefully trained to find it unthinkable. And why? Now that I—we, that is—have thought of it, it seems that there must be more to our dread of the forest floor than just the threat of the Pash-shan. What can be down there that makes it necessary for Kindar not only to stay far above, but even to keep their eyes averted? What can it be that is so evil that we must not even look in its direction?" Leaning forward, Neric pounded his fist on a branch in excitement. "You are right, Raamo. We must go to the forest floor. We will go—on the next free day. And that is only two days from now. We must make our plans very carefully."

There are times when two days can last an eternity, and others when the hours disappear like minutes. The

two days that followed Raamo's meeting with Neric somehow managed to be both. At times Raamo thought the
two days would never end, and at others he was appalled
to realize how little time remained. He slept but little
during the two nights, and when he did sleep, he
dreamed. Each time he sank slowly into restless slumber,
he began to dream—and always it was the same dream.

It began in a dark obscurity that gradually lightened
into drifting gray clouds. As the clouds became less dense,
they were penetrated by dim rays of greenish light, which
made visible a strange scene, a scene muted by thickly
clustering shadows and yet full of strangely distinct and
vivid details.

A wall rose up on the left, a rough bark-covered wall
that seemed to be the trunk of an enormous grundtree.
Near it two huge mushrooms stood like pillars on each
side of a pathway that wound away into a green-tinged
darkness. Standing there, between the mushroom guard
posts, Raamo's dreamself contemplated the winding path
with fear. The fear was sharp and real, as was every detail
of the scene before him. His frightened glance registered
in intricate detail the shade and texture of the earth below
his feet, the pale color of the mushroom columns, and the
small bush, heavy with purple bloom, that stood just to
the right of the pathway.

Then suddenly, out of the greenish shadow ahead,
there came a call for help, and Raamo moved forward into
darkness and fear; and awoke, trembling and wet with
perspiration.

At last the morning of the appointed day dawned, the
special ceremony dedicated to Joy in freedom and relaxation was over, and the free afternoon began. As the other
novices lazed in their nids or gathered for games and

gossip in the common room, Raamo climbed from his balcony to the roof of the novice hall, and from there, by a circuitous route to the meeting place.

When he pushed aside the curtain of Wissenvine, Neric was already there. As Raamo entered, he sprang up, his thin face twitching with excitement.

"Ah, there you are," he said. "I have planned our route to the outskirts of the Temple-grunds. We will—" he stopped as Raamo pushed past him and seated himself on a branch.

"I would like to rest a moment first," Raamo said, "and to hear your news of my sister."

Neric struck his chest in self-reproach. "Forgive me," he said. "In my excitement, I had forgotten for the moment. I have gone to the nid-place of your parents, as I said I would, and I have spoken with your mother—and I have seen your sister." He paused for a moment, and then continued. "She is ill, indeed. She is very pale and thin, and your mother told me that she is no longer able to attend her classes at the Garden. Your mother says that she eats very little—except for Wissenberries."

Raamo shook his head in exasperation. "Why do they permit it?" he said. "I feel sure they do her harm."

"Your mother, I think, agrees with you. But Pomma complains of great pain when she is without the Berry, and her begging weakens your mother's resolve to keep them from her."

Neric's eyes searched Raamo's face, and he put his hand on Raamo's shoulder. "Your sister is still able to leave her nid at times," he said, "and during the ceremony of healing her responses were clear and strong. I think there may still be some—"

"Hope?" Raamo asked.

"Well, yes," Neric said. "If one finds comfort in hoping. But I, for one, find more solace in action. I had meant to say that there might still be some *time*. A little time to search for an answer—a cause—perhaps a cure."

There may be some time—a *little* time—only a little time left for one so young. The thought seemed to drain the brilliance from the sunlit leaves and blossoms and poison the rainwashed air with bitterness. If the source of the evils that were plaguing Green-sky and its innocent inhabitants lay, indeed, with the Pash-shan, Raamo felt that he would be willing to do whatever might be necessary to find the solution, even if the search took him into the very tunnels of the monsters.

"Let us go," he said, and Neric looked at him sharply, surprised at the harshness of his voice.

The pathway lay first along small offshoot branches, through dense growths of leaves and twigs, and finally into the branches of an uninhabited grund that grew on the outskirts of the Temple Grove. Gliding among the branches of the Temple-grunds would have been dangerous, inviting observation by dozens of curious eyes; but here there was little chance of being seen. Raamo and Neric launched themselves into open space and drifted downward.

Unlike the glidepaths in cities and towns, which were carefully cleared and broadened, the route they now followed was narrow and twisting and overgrown with small branches and heavy growths of Vine. Twice they were forced to land and walk until they came to another area open enough for gliding. Soon after the beginning of their third glide, they saw, directly below them, an enormous branch, many feet in diameter and unmistakably a part of the lowest grund-level. Banking sharply, they spiraled down to land on its broad surface. From here to the forest floor, more than a hundred feet below, there were no more branches, but only tree trunks and tangled interwoven growths of Vine. The enormous unbroken surfaces of the grundtrunks were impossible to climb, except when they were strung with ladders as they were between branch levels in the cities. The smooth slender boles of the rooftrees were climbable only by those gifted with strong limbs and a simalike agility at shinnying. So the best route to the forest floor, if one could be found, would be a place where a cluster of Vine stems formed a ladderlike network. A glide to the floor would, of course, be possible but extremely dangerous, since one would land among tall fern, probably far from a means of retreat to the higher levels, and quite possibly very near the mouth of a Pash-shan ventilation tunnel. Walking along the broad branchpath of the forest grund, Raamo and Neric looked carefully for a suitably heavy growth of Vine.

"There," Neric said at last, already whispering although there was as yet no reason for it. "There, that looks climbable." He was pointing to a place where a twisted mass of Wissenvine passed only a few feet from the edge of their branchpath.

Raamo nodded. For only a moment they stood looking downward to where, far below, they could see what seemed to be a solid carpet of shadowy green. And then Raamo jumped, grasping frantically for hand- and footholds in the tangle of Vine. He slipped a few feet, came to a stop, and then began to climb downward. A moment later the Vine vibrated as, above Raamo's head, Neric landed. Glancing up, Raamo saw Neric's foot groping for a foothold directly above his head. Then he gave his full attention to the climb and to the rapidly diminishing distance to the forest floor. He did not stop again until he was directly above the highest fronds of the giant fern.

Dangling from his makeshift Vine ladder, Raamo turned from side to side, his eyes probing every opening in the heavy undergrowth, his ears straining to hear the slightest sound. The ferns seemed to grow in thick clumps. Their curved fronds sprang up, higher than a man's head, and then curved over in graceful arches. Here and there the pale sleek domes of mushrooms loomed almost as tall as the ferns themselves.

A few more steps and Raamo was below the canopy of fronds, and the earth itself was visible. For the most part, it seemed to be carpeted in thick green mosses, but here and there were patches of deep, dark brown. Raamo stared in fascination. The brown surface, rough in texture, rich in hue, warm and damp and pungent, was earth. The earth that nourished everything—and yet threatened everything with its dark mysteries. Raamo was still staring when Neric's foot touched his head.

"Sst," Neric whispered. "Go on. I'm slipping."

A moment later Raamo's foot came in contact with a firm and yet spongy surface, and he was standing on the forest floor. As he turned quickly, alert for the slightest sound or motion, Neric landed beside him with a soft thud. Back to back, poised for instant retreat back up the Wissenvine, they stood for many minutes, immobilized by fear and fascination.

The very air was foreign to them, warmer, and heavy with rich musty odors. There was not the slightest breeze stirring, and the leaves and fronds hung motionless in the deep hush. When a faint rustling noise broke the silence, both Raamo and Neric jumped toward the Wissenvine, before they realized that the sound came from beneath a fallen grundleaf very near their feet. Bending, Raamo jerked the leaf away, and a small creature, no larger than a baby treebear, leaped out and raced away with a strange bounding gait. Grinning sheepishly at each other, they resumed their vigil.

At last Raamo crouched and, reaching out to where the bare earth was visible near the base of a fern clump, he dug with his fingers and then filled his hand with the warm damp soil. Standing again, he examined it closely. Neric, too, bending over Raamo's hand, experimented with it, pressing a small amount into a ball and then crumbling it again with his fingers. Holding it near their faces, they sniffed it, and the strange rich smell moved Raamo with a deep obscure excitement, as if it awakened something within him that had long been forgotten. At last he opened the drawstring on his belt pouch and carefully deposited the earth inside.

"Come on," Neric was whispering. "We won't discover anything by standing here all day. We must find a way to mark our path back to this spot, and then we must start exploring." He reached up and, breaking off a feather of fern, he placed it on the earth in front of them, its tip pointing down the nearest corridor of open space. "Shall we go this way?"

Raamo shrugged to indicate that one way was as good as another, since they had no idea where they were going or even what they were looking for. They started off, slowly and softly, stopping every few yards to deposit another fern frond to mark their path.

The light was dim in the fern-arched corridor. Underfoot the earth was soft and springy—a strange sensation to feet accustomed to the smooth hard surfaces of grundbranches. Unfamiliar insects—fat black beetles and large ants—scurried away before their approach. Here and there delicate white flowers bloomed amid clumps of tiny rounded leaves, while larger bushes bore enormous clusters of red and orange blossoms. Several times they passed large protrusions—masses of some unfamiliar material, gray brown in color and of a strangely hard and cold consistency.

"It is called stone," Neric said. "I have heard of it."

Raamo ran his hands over the cool hardness of the stone. He poked at the black beetles and stooped to smell the flowers. Everywhere he looked were strange and wondrous sights, sights so intriguing that several times he found it necessary to remind himself of the seriousness of their mission—and of the great danger.

A moment later he was forcefully reminded when their path crossed an area where a network of ridges crisscrossed the surface of the earth, making it difficult to walk without tripping. "Is that the Root?" Raamo whispered.

Neric nodded. "I have heard it described by the Vine Priests. It is in areas like this, where the Root grows close to the surface of the soil, that there are most apt to be tunnels." He bent and, picking up a twig, he scratched a thin layer of moss and soil from the top of one of the ridges, revealing a vinelike growth as thick as a man's arm and very much like an old gnarled branch in appearance. But when Raamo touched the Root with his fingers, he snatched them back quickly in shocked surprise. The Root was cold, with a fierce consuming coldness that seemed to grip his fingers and suck at their warmth. Clutching his fingers, he stared at Neric. "Touch it," he said.

"I have heard of its coldness," Neric said. Touching it,

he, too, pulled his hand away swiftly. "It is indeed an enchanted growth."

Suddenly Neric clutched Raamo's arm. "Look," he breathed, pointing toward a thick clump of fern. Drifting up through the fronds, a thick gray haze spiraled into a towering column that stretched up and up, to finally disappear from view among the distant grundbranches.

"A cloud column." Neric's whisper was almost too soft to hear. "We must be near the mouth of a tunnel."

They crept forward, an inch at a time, their bodies turned sideways in preparation for instant flight. Gradually they became aware of a musty acrid odor. As they rounded the base of the fern clump, the smell grew stronger, and Raamo found that his eyes were pained and watering. Panic assailed him as he recalled the stories of the poisonous qualities of the Pash-shan cloud columns, but before he could turn to flee, he saw something that shocked him into immobility. There before his eyes, only a few feet from where he was standing, was a large dark hole. The hole was perhaps a foot across at the widest place. It was bordered by sections of dark gray Root, making it resemble a gray-lipped mouth, and from between these strange lips there issued the thick column of eye-paining graywhite haze.

Easing past Raamo, Neric began to circle the tunnel mouth, silently motioning for Raamo to follow. At a fever pitch of excitement, they continued to circle, their eyes glued to the dark opening. The cloud column twisted slowly upward, but nothing else stirred in the gaping tunnel mouth. When they had circled back to their starting place and retreated to a safe distance, Neric spoke.

"Come," he said. "Let's move on before we are poisoned. We have seen what is to be seen here."

Dropping another fern frond, Neric altered their course in order to skirt the cloud column. They had gone only a short distance when the path curved, leading them close to the trunk of an enormous grund. The path seemed to circle the trunk, and they were halfway around it when Raamo suddenly stopped and stood still. A few feet ahead, Neric heard him gasp and turned back.

"What is it?" Neric asked.

Raamo was standing stiffly, staring down a path that turned off to the right. It was a narrower fainter path, and it led directly between two enormous mushrooms and on into a dense thicket of fern and Vine-stem. The air was suddenly heavy with a sultry sweetness, and Neric realized that the odor was coming from a bush that grew just to the right of the pathway. The bush was heavily covered with bloom of a deep rich shade of purple.

"This is the place," Raamo whispered so softly that Neric was not sure that he had heard correctly.

"The place?" he asked. "What place?"

"In my dream. I dreamed about this place and—" Raamo stopped, listening intently, but there was not the slightest sound.

"And what?" Neric shook Raamo's arm, his round eyes darting nervously.

"There was a call, a cry for help," Raamo said.

"I hear nothing."

"Nor I—no wait!" Shutting out the sensations of eyes and ears, Raamo turned his Spirit-force inward to concentrate on receiving in mind-touch, and almost immediately he became aware of it—a faint and indistinct sending that seemed to come from a great distance. Someone, somewhere was sending a weak and wordless plea for help.

Then, just as in the dream, Raamo plunged forward down the dim pathway.

The path curved and turned, and in the dim light Raamo stumbled frequently, but he scarcely noticed. Nor did he react to the fact that Neric, hurrying after him, was continually grabbing at him and urging him to stop and explain. Everything—Neric, the rough pathway, even the fear that still gripped his chest—faded into the background as the cry for help grew louder and more insistent. They had been running for several minutes when the path broke out of the thicket into a small clearing surrounding an enormous grundtrunk. Cowering against the base of the tree, her face contorted with fear, her arms lifted as if to ward them off, was a small child.

As Raamo's own panic subsided, an urgent curiosity took its place. He stared at the strange sight before him, exchanged bewildered glances with Neric, and stared again. The child still cowered, tears streaming down her face, and her whole body trembling visibly.

She was definitely a Kindar child, perhaps six or seven years of age, and perfectly normal in bodily appearance, except for her unusually dark skin. She was dressed, however, in a very strange fashion. Instead of a silken shuba, she was wearing a close-fitting garment made of material that resembled the fur of an animal. The fur was, in texture, so short and fine, and the garment fit the child's small body so closely, that for a moment Raamo thought it was her own skin. At her throat and from her ears there dangled strands of a hard-surfaced material that Raamo now recognized as metal, and among these strands were sparkling particles that caught the light like sunlit raindrops.

Perhaps it was because her fear was so apparent, so

intense and profound, that it seemed to fill the air around her with a tangible force, that Raamo was slow to realize he was actually pensing her. He knew, of course, that she was frightened; but it took him a little time to realize that his knowledge of her fright was greater and more specific than his eyes and ears could have told him. When he did awaken to the possibility and made a conscious effort to center his Spirit-force on her, he was able to pense clearly that she was begging, pleading, for mercy. He did not pense her pleas in exact words or phrases; but her sending was strong and vivid, and almost without hope.

"Do not fear us," he sent in return. "We will not harm you."

The child continued to cower, but her eyes turned searchingly to his. Stepping closer he took her wrist. She cringed at his touch, but he pressed his palm to hers and repeated the sending. Her eyes searched his, and although she still shrank away from him, her sobs began to slacken.

"Can you pense her?" Neric asked.

Raamo nodded.

"She can speak then?"

"I don't know. I pensed feeling only—no words."

"You know what she is, don't you?" Neric asked. "She must be a slave child. A kidnapped Kindar. She must have been captive since she was a very young infant, poor thing."

"But how is it that she is free now?" Raamo said. "How is it that she is above the Root?"

"I don't know. Unless it is true that the Root is withering, and there is somewhere an opening large enough for a child of her size to pass through. What was it that you pensed?"

"Only that she fears us and begs not to be harmed."

Neric nodded. "We must be very strange and frightening to her. She does not know what we are."

As they were speaking, the girl's eyes darted between their faces. Now, suddenly, she lifted her hand and, pointing at the seal on Neric's shuba, she spoke. Although her voice shook with sobs, and she pronounced her vowels strangely in a slurring singsong, the words were unmistakable. "Are you not Ol-zhaan?" she asked.

Raamo and Neric stared at her in astonishment.

"Yes, we are Ol-zhaan," Neric said. "And are you not a Kindar child who has been held captive by the Pash-shan?" He reached out and put his hand on the girl's head. "You must not fear us," he said. "We are of your kind, and we would not harm you." He turned away to Raamo. "How do you suppose she learned to speak? Unless some of the fallen children have been old enough to have learned speech and have taught the others."

"Or else the Pash-shan speak as we do."

"I suppose that is possible," Neric said. "I can't remember being taught anything concerning their manner of speech. But I had always thought of them as being incapable of speaking as humans do."

It was just then that a small furry creature similar to the one they had seen earlier appeared at their feet and, with one bound, leaped into the child's outstretched arms.

"Look," Raamo said. "It is tame." He crouched, bringing his head to the same level as the child's. Reaching out he touched the soft fur of the little animal. "Is it yours?" he asked, smiling. "What is it called?"

"It's my lapan," she said. "His name is Haba."

"Haba," Raamo repeated, stroking the animal's head. "And what is your name?"

"Teera. My name is Teera."

Neric touched Raamo's shoulder. "Come," he said. "It is not safe here. We must—" he stopped, staring at the little girl in consternation. "What are we to do?" he said. "We can't leave her."

"No," Raamo said, "and it would be wrong to take her with us into danger. I think we must take her to safety as quickly as we can and come back again later to search further."

Neric sighed. "But it will be many days before there is another free time when we can get away and not be missed. And we have learned nothing yet."

"Perhaps we have," Raamo said. He motioned toward the child and, speaking softly behind his hand, said, "She has lived among them, and we have found that she can speak. Who knows what she may be able to tell us?"

"That is true," Neric said. "You are right, Raamo. We will take her back with us, and when she is used to us we will question her carefully and—but where will we take her? If she goes with us to the temple, we will have to explain everything. We will have to admit that we have been to the forest floor. That would ruin everything and might be very dangerous for us all. Unless we could find a deserted chamber and hide her there . . . "

"No," Raamo said. "She would be lonely and afraid. She must be with others who will treat her kindly and—I have it. I know where she can be taken."

CHAPTER FOURTEEN

*I*t *was almost dark* before Raamo and Neric and the slave child, Teera, reached the lowest level of Grandgrund. As they crouched on a leafy side branch within sight of the nid-place of the D'ok family, Raamo's legs were trembling from exhaustion. The journey back from the place where they had found Teera had been unexpectedly difficult and time-consuming.

From the first moment, although they had explained carefully that they were taking her to a safe place where she would be treated kindly, the child had been reluctant to accompany them. She had hung back, refusing to take even the first step, while Raamo and then Neric took turns trying to overcome her fear by telling her about the kind and gentle people who would care for her. She listened and seemed to understand, but said nothing, and continued to pull away from them when they tried gently to lead her away.

At last she said, "Can I take Haba?"

"Haba?" Neric said. "Oh, the little animal? Yes, of course you can take him."

She regarded Neric intently, her long dark-lashed

eyes still liquid from her recent tears. "They won't eat him, will they?"

"Eat him?" Neric's lips curled in disgust. "Eat an animal? Of course not." He turned to look at Raamo, his face contorted with horror and pity.

Giving her pet to Neric to hold, Teera held out her hands to Raamo. "Tell me," she said. "Tell me this way."

With palm and eye touch, Raamo sent, "You and Haba will be welcomed with great kindness. No one in Green-sky would think of eating your pet."

But Teera shook her head, and her return sending was one of bewilderment. Raamo tried again, this time sending only a wordless assurance of truth and good faith. This Teera understood. A tiny smile touched her tear-stained face and, reclaiming her lapan, she at last moved forward.

They walked in single file along the dark thicket pathway, past the cloud-breathing tunnel mouth and then, by following the frond markers, back to the thick stand of Vine-stem down which they had climbed. But having reached the route to safety, they encountered new and unanticipated complications. It was obvious that the makeshift Vine ladder would be hard enough to climb with both hands free, so it was necessary, first of all, to devise some kind of carrier for the lapan. After some experimenting and much looping and tying, the green tabard that marked Raamo as a novice was converted into a carrying pouch large enough to accommodate the small animal.

As Raamo and Neric worked on the pouch, Teera watched with interest but apparently with no understanding of what lay behind their actions. For, when the pouch was finished and the lapan placed inside it, and Raamo began to climb up the Vine, her reaction was shocked surprise—and panic.

"No, no," she cried, when she saw that she was expected to climb behind him. "I cannot. I'm afraid. I will fall."

"Hush! Hush!" Neric whispered, glancing around in fear that her voice might have attracted the attention of the Pash-shan. "Come back down and talk to her, Raamo. She doesn't want to climb."

She would have to climb. There was no other way, since she was too large for them to carry. But convincing the once more tearful Teera of the fact was a long and arduous process. Raamo and Neric argued, reasoned, and reassured in turn, with one of them talking and pleading while the other stood watch, fearfully searching the deepening shadows around them. At last she agreed to try—and the climbing began.

The climb went on—and on—and on. Every few feet Teera would panic and, clutching blindly, would refuse to loosen so much as a finger to reach for the next hold. Then Raamo would have to work his way back down to her—or Neric work his way up—gently loosen her grip and guide her hands upward. Starting, stopping, comforting and cajoling, they progressed a few inches at a time, until at last they reached the level of the first grundbranches. There another crisis occurred.

In the lead, Raamo had climbed up to a level slightly above the branch and then glided easily down to light on its broad surface. But when he stood at the edge and reached out toward Teera, she refused to jump the small gap between their reaching hands. It was not until he had collected some Vine tendrils, which Neric then tied carefully around her waist, that he was able to pull her across to safety.

Collapsed on the broad surface of the deserted grundbranch, Neric stared at the still sobbing Teera. "Great Sorrow!" he exclaimed. "I almost wish we'd left her to the mercy of the Pash-shan. I'm exhausted."

"And I also," Raamo said. "But her fear is to be expected, I suppose. Openness and heights are as frightening to her as dark airless tunnels would be to us. And perhaps in the depths of her mind there is some memory of her fall to the forest floor. She was probably injured by the fall—and then to have been seized and pulled down into the earth by such fearful creatures—it is no wonder that the fear of falling causes her such great mindpain."

"True," Neric said, grinning ruefully. "There can be no doubt that fear can cause great mind-pain, and other pains as well." Gingerly he touched a bruised and swollen lip with the tip of his finger. "On the Vine," he explained in answer to Raamo's questioning look, "during one of her spasms of mind-pain, she kicked me full in the mouth." He rose to his feet, sighing. "We still have to get her down some narrow sidebranches if we are to reach your parents' nid-place unobserved. We had best be going. Darkness will soon be upon us."

Thus it was that Raamo and Neric and a weary tearstained girl child crouched behind sheltering grundleaves and watched the last straggling Kindar hurrying to their nid-places as darkness fell. When the branchpath was at last deserted, they struggled to their feet and, with Teera between them, hurried down the branch and burst into the common room of the D'ok nid-place.

The room was empty, but sounds of voices came from

the hall leading to the pantry. Raamo recognized his mother's voice and that of the helper, Ciela.

"I will take Teera to Pomma's chamber," he whispered. "When we are gone, you call and announce your presence to my mother. Then bring her with you to Pomma's chamber."

If Hearba was surprised to find the young priest of healing, D'ol Neric, in her common room so close to the time of rainfall, she carefully hid it, out of politeness and respect. But when, on entering her daughter's chamber, she found Raamo, holding Pomma in his arms, with a weirdly clad girl child standing beside him, her careful calm was lost completely—first to Joy, and then to shock and consternation.

"Raamo," she cried joyously and then, "Why are you here? You were not to visit us during the first year of your novitiate. What is it? What has happened?"

There was no time for lengthy explanations. There was no time even to call Valdo D'ok from his nid-chamber where he was resting before the evening food-taking. Neric explained briefly that the girl had been a slave of the Pash-shan, only recently rescued, and that she must be sheltered and kept secure and secret until such time as he or Raamo returned for her.

Keeping his face under strict control, forcing a false smile to hide his grief over her worsened condition, Raamo hugged Pomma a last time and carried her back to her nid. "Remember, Pomma," he whispered, "I will need your help in keeping Teera's presence a secret. And in keeping her content and happy here in our home."

"Is she really going to stay here with us?" Pomma asked. "Is she to live here with me in my chamber?"

Raamo nodded.

"But what of Ciela?" Hearba asked. "She will surely have to see the child."

"I will speak to her now," Neric said. "I will tell her the child's presence here is approved by the Ol-zhaan, and that she must not speak of it to anyone. But Ciela must not see you here, Raamo, so while I am speaking to her, you must wait for me in the entryway. We must hurry, for we have far to go if we are to approach the Temple-grove from the outer forest. And the rain has already begun."

Turning to his mother, Raamo took time for only the briefest palm-touch before he hurried across the common room and out into the darkness and softly falling rain.

The journey back to the grove was long, uncomfortable and frightening. Stumbling through the wet darkness along slippery branchpaths, Raamo and Neric finally arrived on the outskirts of the grove, just in time to be trapped there by a belated group of Ol-zhaan making their way from the great hall to their chambers. At last the stragglers disappeared and, waving a silent good-bye to Neric, Raamo made his way across the public branchpath and darted into the branchends, where Neric's secret route led him to the roof of the novice hall. A few minutes later he dropped softly down onto the balcony of his chamber and crept wet and trembling through the window.

A dozen days passed before another free afternoon made it possible for Raamo to return again, secretly, to the house of his parents. In the meantime, however, Neric was able to visit the D'ok's nid-place three times, as a part of his ministry of healing in the city of Orbora. Following each of these visits he was able to arrange brief meetings with Raamo to tell him what he had learned.

"You should see her," he told Raamo, during a meeting in their trysting place behind the curtain of Vine near the Temple Hall. "They have dressed her in one of your sister's shubas and arranged her hair more normally, and one would scarcely notice her on any branchpath in Green-sky, except of course, if she spoke—with that strange slurring accent of hers. Even her skin seems to be a more normal shade now. Do you know what she says caused its darkness?"

Raamo shook his head.

"The sunlight," Neric said, his lifted eyebrows inviting Raamo to share his incredulous reaction. "I was sure she was speaking an untruth at first. But then she explained that all Erdlings—a term she apparently uses to mean both Pash-shan and Kindar slaves—spend many hours daily in the areas where the tunnels run between the aisle of the orchard trees. And the sun, she says, falling down between the grillwork of Root, quickly turns skin to that strange golden hue."

"But what does she say of the Pash-shan?" Raamo asked.

Neric shook his head, sighing. "Very little, I'm afraid. She speaks to me quite freely now concerning many things, but when I mention the Pash-shan, she stares at me strangely and begins to tremble. She must be deathly afraid of the very memory of them, poor child. I will be glad when the next free day comes and you can accompany me to your parents' home to question her. Perhaps by pensing, you will be able to learn more."

"You have learned nothing then, concerning the Pash-shan?"

"A little. I learned for instance that they are indeed flesheaters, as we have been told. Teera told me that much when I questioned her concerning her escape. She said that she had run away from the Pash-shan because they were going to eat her pet, the small creature she calls Haba. She said she was trying to find a hiding place, and was wandering down ventilation tunnels far from her living place, when she discovered a spot where the Root left an opening large enough for her to squeeze through. She put the lapan through the hole first and then followed it, although the cold of the Root was painful and frightening. Then the lapan ran from her, and in following it she became lost and could not find the tunnel opening again. I think she must have been wandering for at' least two days when we found her."

"Do you think she speaks truthfully?" Raamo asked.

"I think so," Neric said, "for the most part, at least. But not freely. She obviously dislikes my questions, and answers as briefly as possible. But she does answer—unless I question her directly about the Pash-shan."

It was some days later that Raamo, leaving his last class of the day and starting back toward the novice hall with Genaa, encountered Neric on the central platform of the grove. Neric hurried past, pretending to be engrossed in private thought, but his sending was clear and urgent and charged with excitement. "Meet me at the hiding place. I have much to tell you."

Raamo continued on some distance before he turned to go back, telling Genaa that he had forgotten a book that D'ol Regle had promised to loan him for the evening.

When he pushed his way through the Wissenvine curtain, Neric sprang to meet him.

"I have news," he said, "concerning the Pash-shan and—" he lowered his voice, "—and I think, the Geets-kel. I was again today at the nid-place of your parents and again questioned the slave child, Teera. I questioned her concerning the cloud columns of the Pash-shan, and she seemed surprised, amused even, that I considered them to be poisonous—and produced by the Pash-shan in order to carry evil and noxious vapors into Green-sky. I was speaking of the cloud column that we saw coming from the tunnel near where we found her, and she said, 'Cloud column? Oh, you mean the smoke.' And then she went on to explain that—"

Suddenly interrupting himself, Neric asked, "Have you learned yet about fire, in your study of preflight history with D'ol Regle?"

"Yes," Raamo said. "Only a few days ago D'ol Regle spoke at great length concerning fire and how it had been a blessing and a curse to our ancestors and how the first Ol-zhaan had banished it from Green-sky."

"Yes, exactly," Neric said. "And the child, Teera, described fire to me much as D'ol Regle did, likening it to dancing petals of sunlight that produce warmth and light—and great pain, if touched. According to her telling, the Pash-shan make use of it for many purposes, but in particular in the preparation of flesh for food. The flesh is heated until it withers and turns dark, and then it is eaten while it is still hot." Neric's lips curled in disgust as he spoke, and Raamo felt his own stomach convulse in rebellion. "The fires of the Pash-shan, Teera says, are fed by lumps of black material that is dug from deep tunnels," Neric went on. "It is also necessary to the production of different kinds of metals, such as that used in the ornaments she was wearing when we found her. However—" And here Neric paused to lend significance to what he was about to say. "However—Teera insists that a cloud column produced by fire, or smoke as she calls it, is not poisonous or even harmful unless breathed in an enclosed place, and that although the Pash-shan and captured Kindar always live near fire, they are not harmed by it." Neric leaned forward sharply and lowered his voice. "This, I think, is of great significance. *Why* are we told that the cloud columns are poisonous vapors produced by the Pash-shan to bring harm, if in fact they are only smoke? I am sure the Geets-kel are behind this falsehood for some reason of their own."

Raamo nodded. "Perhaps," he said. "It is certainly *not* that the Geets-kel do not know that the Pash-shan are able to make fire, because D'ol Regle spoke of their use of it. He told us that fire lives by consuming certain materials such as plant life of all kinds, and Genaa asked if the Root could not then be destroyed by fire also. But D'ol Regle said that it could not because it was not a natural growth, but an enchanted one—and if it were not so the Pash-shan would long since have destroyed it and escaped into Green-sky."

"Ah," Neric said, "that, too, is of significance." He pondered for a moment, and then, suddenly rousing himself, he said, "but I am forgetting other news, good news. Your sister, Pomma. Her condition seems to be somewhat improved. Your mother says she has begun to eat a little more, and she seems a little stronger. On my last visit I found her sitting on the floor of her chamber trying to teach Teera the game of Five-Pense."

Raamo's heart seemed to float upward as if a dark

weight had been removed. "I thank you. I thank you, Neric, for this news," he said.

"It is most welcome news for me, also," Neric said. "And not only for the sake of your sister, but for my own sake, also. I had long ago decided that my Ceremonies of Healing were of little use, but now I begin to wonder if I may not have, after all, some slight Spirit-force for healing. It gives me great happiness to think that it may be so."

Raamo rose and moved toward the curtain of Vine. "I had best be going," he said. "I am expected at the novice hall, and my absence might arouse some curiosity. I will meet you here again on the free day, right after the ceremony."

"Good," Neric said. "Teera has asked about you. I think she feels more at ease in your presence than in mine. I am expecting much from your next meeting with her. I am sure that we will learn many things concerning the Pash-shan when you next meet her."

"I hope so—" Raamo was beginning when he paused suddenly with his hand lifted for silence. "What was that?" he asked.

"What was what?" Neric said.

"I heard a rustling—" Raamo parted the thick sheltering leaves of the Vine and looked out toward the branch-path. There was no one in sight. "That's strange," he said. "I was sure I heard—or felt—a presence other than our own."

"Perhaps it was a trencher bird," Neric said. "There are many in this part of the grove."

"Perhaps," Raamo said. "Until the free day then, Peace and Joy to you."

"And Joy to you, Raamo," Neric said, offering his palms.

"But not Peace?" Raamo asked, smiling.

"But not Peace," Neric said. "May we not accept the comfort of peaceful minds until we have discovered the secret of the Geets-kel."

CHAPTER FIFTEEN

*T**he days that followed** passed very swiftly. For the first time in many weeks, the knowledge of Pomma's illness no longer haunted the quiet corners of Raamo's days. He attended his classes with renewed interest and began to find himself looking forward to some of them, in particular his daily meeting with the ancient D'ol Falla.

D'ol Falla lived in the most magnificent living chambers in the entire grove. These chambers, which according to legend had been originally constructed for D'ol Wissen himself and had for many generations been the dwelling place of the high priest of the Vine, were splendid examples of the skill and artistry of Kindar architecture. Beginning in a large and lavish reception hall, just to the east of the central platform of the grove, the chambers ranged upward, so skillfully supported and suspended that they seemed almost to be floating—a drift of large airy chambers connected by hallways woven of hardened tendril—mellowed by time to a smooth ivory-hued filigree and interwoven with living honey-vine. Covered rampways ascended between levels, and beautifully fashioned Vine-screens enclosed the entire area, giving unity and privacy to the enormous dwelling-place.

It was here Raamo came daily, either alone or with D'ol Druvo, the third-year novice who was also preparing for service as a priest of the Vine. In a small chamber off the large reception hall, D'ol Falla would be waiting. She was always there when Raamo entered, seated in a large thronelike chair of woven tendril.

She was a tiny woman, as thin and sere as a dry leaf. So fragile did she appear that one almost feared to touch her palms in greeting lest they crumble away at contact. The skin of her face was webbed with a delicate network of tiny wrinkles, but her legendary beauty was still evident in the proportion of her features and the intense vitality of her astonishingly youthful green eyes.

In her high whispery voice she spoke to Raamo of many things that were of deep and consuming interest to him. She spoke of D'ol Wissen, the first priest of the Vine, of the forest floor, of the Root, and sometimes of the Pash-shan. As she spoke, her eyes probed into Raamo's and at times he felt the faintest whisper of mind-touch, as if blind and blunted Spirit fingers were prying at the edges of his mind. The whisper intrigued him, tempted him to release his careful mind-blocking and center his Spirit-force in a response so strong that the barrier would fall away and the silent whisper would reveal its secrets. But remembering Neric's warning about D'ol Falla, that she was among the Geets-kel, Raamo resisted the temptation and only watched and listened.

If Raamo was greatly interested in every mention made by D'ol Falla of the Pash-shan, there was one whose interest seemed to be even greater than his own. Every evening when Raamo had returned from D'ol Falla's class,

Genaa was waiting for him with many questions. As she listened to every word, to every scrap of information, Genaa's dark eyes glowed with a bright intensity that was almost frightening. And when Raamo was slow to answer or had little to impart, she quickly became impatient.

"Is that all?" she would say. "Surely she has told you more than that by now. If only my request had been granted and I had been the one to be assigned as Vine priest!"

On the next free day, thirteen days after Teera had been placed in the custody of the D'ok family, Raamo and Neric met again in their secret hiding place. The morning ceremony was over, and the rest of the day was theirs. Immediately, by hidden sidebranch and then by open forest, they began their long roundabout journey to the lower level of Grandgrund. Approaching cautiously, they crept through Vine-growths and leafy branchends until they came to the spot where they had waited on the night they brought Teera to the D'ok nid-place. Even now, with no strangely attired slave child in their company, it was of the greatest importance that they not be observed. The rule that prohibited a novice Ol-zhaan from visiting his family during the first year of his novitiate was well known to all Kindar. Hidden behind a large cluster of grundleaves, they watched and waited until the branch-path was free of strolling Kindar, and then they walked swiftly to the doorway of the D'ok nid-place.

Since they had been warned by Neric on his last visit, the D'ok family was expecting their arrival. They were waiting, gathered together in the common room, when Raamo and Neric threw back the door hangings and rushed into the room. For a moment all was a confusion of joyous cries and hastily sung greetings. Valdo, Hearba and Pomma, too, crowded around Raamo, pressing their palms to his and laughing with Joy. It was several minutes before the uproar subsided enough for Raamo to make use of his eyes with understanding.

The first thing he saw clearly, and with great happiness, was Pomma. Dressed in a new shuba of blending golds and pinks, she stood before him glowing like a moonmoth. Her lovely eyes shone with Joy at Raamo's presence, and her cheeks pulsed with color. She was still painfully thin and her pale skin still seemed to be almost transparent, but the change for the better was undeniable.

"See how much better I am, Raam—, I mean D'ol Raamo. Look how much fatter." Pomma held out her still pitifully thin arms proudly. "And Teera, too." Running back to where Teera watched shyly from the hallway, Pomma pulled her forward. "Look how much fatter Teera is. Teera loves to eat. She likes eggs best, but she loves to eat everything. She hadn't ever tasted eggs before or tree mushrooms either, but she likes them very much. Mother says she's never seen a child eat as much as Teera does."

Stooping to put himself at the child's level, Raamo held out his palms to Teera, and she responded hesitantly. She did, indeed, seem healthier and stronger, and her expressive full-lipped face was more rounded.

"Peace and Joy to you, Teera," he said, and then to Pomma, "It is not to be wondered at that Teera was hungry when she came to you. She had been wandering without anything to eat for two days when we found her."

"I know," Pomma said. "And before that, too, she was hungry. Teera says that everyone is hungry below the Root."

Raamo and Neric exchanged quick glances, but before Raamo could question Teera, Pomma went on.

"Teera likes everything to eat except Berries. She doesn't like Berries at all. Isn't that funny?"

"I like them," Teera said, in her soft slurring voice. "I like the taste of them, but I don't like the way they make me feel. They make me feel dizzy—like looking down and thinking I might fall. The Berries make me feel like falling."

Pomma giggled. "Teera likes to play games," she said. "I've been teaching her games and songs. I've taught her the Rain Song and the Naughty Bear. And she already knew how to play Hide-and-Find and Toss-Up, just like we do. And soon, when I'm better and when Teera doesn't have to be a secret anymore, I'm going to teach her how to glide and climb and we're going to go beak-hunting together. And do you know what, Raamo? We can even play Five-Pense together."

Raamo laughed, delighted at his sister's enthusiasm and amused by her exaggeration.

"Five-Pense?" he asked. "Even Five-Pense? Aren't you overspeaking just a little?"

Five-Pense, a game that was revered as symbolic of all the beauties of childhood, depended on mind-touch, and progressed through five levels of communication, each one requiring greater Spirit-force and mind-response. It was played, usually, only by the very young, and certainly not by children of Pomma's age, who had long been unable to pense.

"No," Pomma said. "I'm not overspeaking. We can truly. I thought I was too old, too, but Teera and I *can* pense each other. We can do Signals and Choices all the time, and sometimes we can do Images. We can't do Four and Five yet, but I think we're going to. Isn't that wonderful?"

Neric caught Raamo's eye and, making very obvious signals, he said, "Pomma, would you come sit here by me for a while. I would like to speak to you, and I think D'ol Raamo would like to speak privately with Teera for a few moments." He jerked his head in the direction of Pomma's chamber. "Wouldn't you like to speak to Teera, D'ol Raamo?"

"Yes, I would," Raamo said. "Teera, would you come with me?"

He reached for her hand to lead her out of the room, but she shrank back. "To ask me questions?" she asked. "You want to ask me questions?"

Instead of answering, Raamo captured the child's nervously fluttering hands and with palm- and eye-touch he sent a wordless reassurance of comfort and goodwill. The fear clouding Teera's eyes cleared slowly and at last she nodded.

"If you will pardon," Raamo said to Hearba and Valdo. "I would like to speak to Teera alone for a few minutes."

But as Raamo turned to go, the door hangings in the front entry were suddenly flung aside and a voice said, "And I, too, would like to speak to Teera."

It was Genaa D'anhk. Standing framed in the arch of the doorway, Genaa had never looked lovelier, or more intimidating. She stood tall and straight, graceful and yet commanding, the rich luxury of her beauty contrasting strangely with something starkly narrow and rigid in her manner, and in the intensity with which she stared at Teera. Brushing aside the greeting of Raamo's parents with the slightest of gestures, Genaa moved forward, and Raamo found himself moving, with her, toward the hallway that led to Pomma's chamber.

Inside the chamber, Genaa began at once to question Teera, who was once more cringing and trembling.

"I wish to speak to you of the Pash-shan," Genaa said to the child. "What do they look like? Can they speak? Why do they persecute the Kindar?"

Shrinking back against the wall, Teera covered her face with her hands. "I don't know," she sobbed. "I can't tell you about them. I can't. I can't."

"You can't what? Why can't you tell us about them? They can't harm you here. What are you afraid of?"

Genaa was holding Teera firmly by both shoulders, but the child seemed to be wilting in her grasp, so weakened by fear that she appeared to be on the point of collapse. At last Raamo intervened. Pulling Genaa away, he spoke to her softly.

"She can tell us nothing when she is so frightened. I think we must begin slowly."

"But why is she so afraid? What is it that she fears?"

"I don't know," Raamo said. "Us, partly, I think. I think she fears Ol-zhaan."

"And the Pash-shan? Is it her memories of the Pash-shan that frightens her so when they are mentioned?"

"Perhaps," Raamo said. "There is something very strange there. But if we are to find out anything, we must go very slowly. I have tried to question her before, and Neric has several times, and we have learned that we must be very slow and gentle and speak first of other things."

Genaa nodded, and approaching the child again she began to talk to her concerning the games she played with Pomma. But Teera continued to sob, refusing even to remove her hands from her tear-wet face. The crying went on and on, and Genaa's questions were again betraying her impatience, when Pomma suddenly appeared in the doorway. Frowning, she went to Teera and put her arms around her.

"Go away, Raamo," she said, forgetting the deference that was now due her brother. "Go away and take her with you." She pointed to Genaa.

"Come, Genaa," Raamo said. "Pomma will be able to quiet her. We can try again later."

Surprisingly, Genaa followed without protest as Raamo returned to the common room. Neric was alone in the large room, pacing up and down the floor, his thin face twitching with emotion.

"Where are my parents?" Raamo asked.

"I asked them to leave us for a time," Neric said. "It seems we have things to speak of, the three of us." Turning to Genaa, he asked, "Why are you here? You know you are not permitted to leave the grove unless directed to do so by an elder."

Genaa's smile was sharply edged. "That is true," she said, "and true also of Raamo, I think. I am here because I followed you. And I followed you today because several days ago I followed Raamo when he went to meet you near Temple Hall. I waited nearby and heard you speak of the slave child and what you were learning from her concerning the Pash-shan. And so I decided that I would also question this child who has lived with the monsters, as it is of great importance to me to learn all I can of them."

"And what, then, did you learn from Teera, with your superior methods of questioning?" Neric's voice bit like the edge of a trencher's beak.

Genaa shrugged, her color rising. "Nothing. She would not stop crying long enough to talk."

Neric threw up his arms in exasperation. "See. What

did I tell you?" he said to Raamo. "This one will bring us nothing but trouble. The child was beginning to speak quite freely to me, and I'm sure she would willingly have told you almost anything, had you been alone, Raamo. But now the day is probably wasted."

"It will not be wasted for me," Genaa said, "if you and Raamo will tell me what it is that you are doing—and how it concerns the Pash-shan. And who are the Geets-kel, of whom you spoke?"

Raamo looked at Neric. Remembering Neric's reaction when he had suggested that they tell Genaa of their plans and ask her to join them, Raamo was surprised to see him shrug.

"You agree, then?" he asked. "You agree to sharing what we have learned with Genaa and asking her to help us?"

Neric sighed loudly. "I agree to telling her what she wants to know, since she seems to have learned much of it already. And I agree that we must then ask her cooperation, at least to the extent of not betraying us to the Geets-kel. As for asking her to help us—you see how she has helped us today, with her skillful interrogation of the slave child."

Inexplicably, Genaa responded to the biting tone of Neric's words with a smile that was open and conciliatory. The smile changed Genaa, softening grandeur into charm, and it seemed to change Neric, too, transforming his bitter opposition into a very uncharacteristic state of uncertainty. "I'm sorry," Genaa said, "about frightening the child. I see now that I acted too hastily. It is a fault of mine. It would have been much better to let Raamo speak to her alone. If you will tell me what you have learned, I promise that—that I will not act hastily on what I learn.

And as for betraying you—I do not know you well, D'ol Neric, but I know Raamo well enough to be certain that he would not be involved in anything evil. I will not betray a cause that Raamo believes in."

So Genaa was told everything. Neric began by describing his early disillusionment and the accident that had placed him in the secret chamber where the Geets-kel were meeting. Genaa listened carefully, and when Neric spoke of what he had overheard concerning the Pashshan—that the Geets-kel seemed to know of some terrible secret concerning the Pash-shan, which in some mysterious way threatened all life on Green-sky, she leaned forward sharply, her long dark eyes fixed and staring.

Then Raamo explained how Neric had contacted him and asked his assistance in discovering the secret, and how they had together planned the trip to the forest floor, and what had occurred there.

When at last the telling was finished, Neric, smiling his crooked smile, turned to Genaa. "And now, D'ol Genaa," he said, "we shall see if I was right when I once told Raamo that you would not sacrifice pride and power for any cause, and that you were at heart, if not yet in reality, among the Geets-kel. Now that you know our secrets—and the full extent of our transgressions—will you join us, or the Geets-kel?"

"You do not know me as well as you think, D'ol Neric," Genaa said. "There is a cause for which I would sacrifice pride and power and much else besides. And that is—to free Green-sky from the curse of the Pash-shan. If you are correct in thinking that the Geets-kel are in some way in league with the Pash-shan, it seems to me that my cause and yours are one. I will gladly work with you to uncover the secret for which you are searching."

At that moment, Pomma reentered the room from the hallway that led to her chamber.

"Where is Teera?" Raamo asked. "How is she?"

"She is sleeping," Pomma said. "She cried for a long time and then she went to sleep, so I came back to see you." Carrying her sima on her shoulder, Pomma crossed the room and climbed into Raamo's lap where she snuggled sleepily.

Neric returned to his conversation with Genaa. "I'm sure the secret lies with the Pash-shan," he said. "Raamo and I have discussed several methods of finding out more about them. We have tried to make use of Raamo's skills. He has let it be known that his Spirit-skills are failing, in order to put them off their guard, and he has attempted pensing whenever he is near any whom we suspect to be of the Geets-kel."

"I understand now," Genaa said to Raamo, "about your telling D'ol Regle you could no longer pense. Have you learned anything of importance?"

"Very little," Raamo said. "All of the Ol-zhaan seem to be very careful to mind-block at all times. There have been times with D'ol Falla when I thought I could almost hear—but it was not certain. And I was once able to pense quite clearly that D'ol Regle opposed my choosing and was almost afraid of me."

"There must be more that can be done," Genaa said.

"There is," Neric said, "and we have tried it once and will go again. We plan to—" he broke off, looking at Pomma.

Raamo glanced down. Curled in his lap, Pomma's eyes were closed and she was breathing regularly. "She is sleeping," he sent to Neric, and Neric nodded. Lowering his voice, he continued, "We plan other trips to the forest floor. I feel certain there is much to be learned there. We were not able to explore very much on our first attempt, because of finding Teera."

"I will go with you when you go again," Genaa said. "And there may be other things that I can do. There are clues, I am certain, in even the little you have learned so far. Little things, little facts that could be strung together into meaning. I am very good at such things." She glanced from Raamo to Neric and back again. "I think," she said, smiling, "that, working together, we will be invincible. We seem to complement each other's talents. Together I am certain we will soon learn everything about the Pash-shan. Not only their relationship to the Geets-kel, but also the source of their power, what they really look like and—"

"What the Pash-shan look like?" It was Pomma, still curled in Raamo's lap but with eyes wide open and suspiciously unclouded by sleep. "I already know what the Pash-shan look like. They look just like Teera. I know they look like Teera, because Teera is a Pash-shan."

CHAPTER SIXTEEN

I *f the tallest grundtree* in the forest had crashed to the earth, the sound of its falling could have produced no greater reaction. For several seconds after Pomma's sweet thin voice had died away into silence, her three listeners stared at her in stunned silence. It was Neric who found his voice first.

"She is speaking untruthfully," he said, "or else she is only game playing, as children do."

"No," Raamo said. "She at least believes it to be true." Lifting Pomma off his lap so that he could look into her face, he asked, "Who told you this? Who told you that Teera is a Pash-shan?"

But now Pomma would only hang her head without answering. Raamo had to repeat his question several times before she whispered, "I promised I wouldn't tell, and I forgot." She began to sob. "I really did forget. I forgot I promised Teera I wouldn't tell. She made me promise because she said you and D'ol Neric would dead her if you knew—only she calls it kill. Teera says you and D'ol Neric would kill her because you are Ol-zhaan, and the Ol-zhaan want to kill all the Pash-shan. She said you would have killed her before except you thought she was a fallen Kindar and not a Pash-shan. I told her and told her that you wouldn't, but she wouldn't believe me. Maybe if *you* told her that you wouldn't dead her, she'll believe me and she won't be unjoyful at me for forgetting my promise."

Genaa interrupted Pomma's sobbing entreaty, speaking deliberately in clipped controlled syllables. "Then it was Teera, herself, who told you that she was a Pash-shan?"

Leaning shyly against her brother, Pomma answered: "Not at first. At first she said that there weren't any Pash-shan. That there were just people who live below the Root who look almost the same as Kindar, only they call themselves Erdlings. But then she said that the Erdlings are the same as the Pash-shan. She said the Pash-shan is the name the Ol-zhaan gave them, and the Ol-zhaan keep them shut up below the Root because they want them to die, and all the Erdlings are very very afraid of the Ol-zhaan."

"Surely Teera does not believe that I would harm her," Raamo said. "I have told her in mind-touch of my feelings toward her."

"Yes," Pomma said. "She says she thinks you do not want to hurt her, but she thinks the others might make you do it anyway. She is still afraid of D'ol Neric. And—" Looking toward Genaa, Pomma blushed, and then whispered into Raamo's ear. "And, just now, when she was crying, she said that she was sure that D'ol Genaa would kill her. She said she could pense it."

Pomma's whisper carried well, and Genaa easily overheard. "That's ridiculous," she said, "I had no ill feelings toward her. This proves that she is capable of telling untruths."

"Perhaps not," Raamo said. "I have discovered that Teera can pense quite well, but only emotions and states of mind. She does not receive words or any fine distinctions. If there was ill will in your mind toward anyone, she might well have felt it as a threat."

It was then that Neric jumped suddenly to his feet. "This explains it," he cried. "This explains everything. This is the secret of the Geets-kel. It must have been the Geets-kel who imprisoned the Pash-shan and who are now desperately afraid of their escape. Of course they would be. If all the Kindar knew that the Pash-shan, the monsters whom they have been taught to fear for so many generations, were only Kindar like themselves whose ancestors were imprisoned by the Ol-zhaan—if the Kindar were to find out that the gentle justice of the Ol-zhaan included a dungeon full of innocent descendants of those who somehow incurred the displeasure of the great and godlike Ol-zhaan—what would happen then?"

"Can it be true?" Raamo asked. "But why? Why should they do such a thing?"

"Who knows," Neric said. "It must have been accomplished before the final spreading of the Root. Perhaps the first prisoners were those who disagreed with the policies of the early Ol-zhaan."

"D'ol Regle said there was a disagreement among the early Ol-zhaan," Raamo said. "He called it a debate. It concerned who should be told the full history of our ancestors and who should be kept in innocence."

"A debate," Neric laughed scornfully. "A debate in which the losers were doomed to imprisonment below the earth."

"How do you know that the first Pash-shan were undeserving of their fate?" Genaa asked. "Perhaps they were not just those who disagreed. Perhaps they were those who could not be freed from the evil seeds of violence—perhaps they were those who—" Genaa paused, blushing, "—who killed."

Neric had returned to pacing up and down the floor. Now he whirled to face Genaa. "What if they were? You forget they lived hundreds of years ago, my dear Genaa. Why should their descendants suffer for the deeds of their long-forgotten ancestors? They cannot all be evil."

Neric paused dramatically, and in the pause Pomma said, "Teera isn't evil."

"Exactly," Neric shouted, piercing the air with his finger. "Teera is not evil and there must be hundreds of Teeras below the Root, doomed to live out their days in the dark cramped tunnels of the—"

Opening her eyes wide in a mockery of admiring awe, Genaa said, "Your eloquence, D'ol Neric, rivals that of the master, D'ol Regle."

Neric glared, and then turned his back on her.

"There is another thing that puzzles me," Raamo said. "If it is true that there are no Pash-shan, and only Erdlings whose ancestors were Kindar, and if it is true that Teera is such a one, then why did she run away from her own people? And why did she agree to come with us to the upper levels?"

"Yes," Genaa said. "Unless she is indeed a fallen Kindar child. There can be no doubt that the Pash-shan steal Kindar infants who fall to the forest floor. Whether they are monsters in shape and form or only in deed, they do *indeed* steal Kindar infants. There is hardly a Kindar in all Green-sky who does not know of at least one family who has lost a child in this way. Undoubtedly the family who cared for her were cruel to her, or she would not have run from their care."

"Did Teera speak to you of this?" Raamo asked Pomma. "Did she say why it was that she ran away?"

"Yes," Pomma said. "She said why. But it was not because she was a fallen. She says she was born below the Root, and she lived there with her father and mother. She said she ran away because her father was going to kill Haba, to eat." Pomma's face twisted in disgust. "She said that all the Erdlings eat lapans. She even has herself, only not pet ones. Teera said she has had Haba for a long time, and her father did not want to eat him, except that they were all very hungry. Teera says that everyone is hungry now below the Root, because too many babies have been born and there is not enough food anymore. But she would never eat Haba even if she were starving, so she took him and ran away. She says she was angry—that's like unjoyful, only worse—with her father when she ran away, only she isn't anymore, and she cries at night because she can't ever go home. And one night she tried to run away from here and go back, but she was afraid of falling so she came back."

"So it is true that they are flesheaters," Genaa said. "And did Teera speak to you of the Kindar infants whom they have taken?"

"Yes," Pomma said. "I asked her about it, and she said that sometimes the babies who fall die, unless the Erdlings take them below the Root, because the Ol-zhaan who come to look for fallen babies come too late or can't find them. So the Erdlings call to the babies, and if they come near the tunnels, and if they are small enough, they take them down to live with them. Teera says her grand-mother was a fallen."

"But the Pash—the Erdlings, do they eat other flesh besides lapan?" Neric asked.

"Birds, I think," Pomma said. "Some kind of birds that live on the forest floor and don't fly. Sometimes they set traps for the birds at the mouths of the tunnels, but they don't catch very many. And they eat mush-rooms, too, big black ones that grow under the ground, and roots of plants, and whatever falls down from the trees in the orchards to where they can reach it. But Teera says there are too many Erdlings now, and there is never enough food and she's been hungry lots and lots of times. She says she'd like to stay here forever and ever because we have so much to eat, and because of me, only she feels so unjoyful about not seeing her own family again."

"What is it like to live below the Root?" Raamo asked. "What can it be like to sleep and wake and live out your days in deep dark holes?"

"Teera says there are big open places called caverns as big as—as big as a grund," Pomma said, "with great high roofs that are covered with sparkles like raindrops, and there are big places of water, and it isn't dark because of a thing called fire that is like little pieces of the sun, and sometimes there is light from tunnel openings. And every family has small caverns all around the big ones that are like nid-places, only their nids are made from the skins of animals. And every day, Teera says, everyone spends some time in the orchard tunnels, where they can feel the sunlight on their skin while they watch for fallen fruits and nuts." Pomma's eyes were shining with excitement and her small hands gestured wildly as she spoke, as if painting on the air the scenes she was describing. "I know just what it looks like," she said, "because Teera has shown me by imagining, but I'd like to really see it, wouldn't you, Raamo? Wouldn't you like to go there to see it?"

"Pomma," Neric interrupted, "would you go back to your chamber now and stay with Teera for a while. We will speak to you again before we go."

When Pomma had obediently left the common room, Neric turned to Raamo in great agitation. "Do you understand," he said, "the significance of what we have just heard? Do you realize the danger we have put your sister in by exposing her to the knowledge she now has? Has it occurred to you what a threat Pomma is now to the Geets-kel, and how necessary it would be to them to silence her if they knew? Only think. A Kindar child, a talkative intelligent Kindar child, knows the secret they have protected so well for hundreds of years. If they feel justified in keeping hundreds of people imprisoned, and thousands more in ignorance, in order to protect their evil secret, how much do you think Pomma's welfare would mean to them?"

"You may be right," Raamo said, "I don't know. I cannot think they would harm Pomma—"

"Fool," Neric said. "You are a fool, Raamo."

"Perhaps," Raamo said. "But what can we do? How can we protect her?"

"I don't know," Neric said. "First, of course, we must warn her to be silent. We must impress on her the necessity of absolute silence concerning what she has heard. And I can tell your mother that she must not yet be allowed to return to her classes at the Garden. With less contact with other children, she will be less tempted to reveal what she has learned. And then we must plan. We must begin to plan what can be done to overcome the power of the Geets-kel and—to free the Erdlings."

"But how can we do that?" Raamo asked. "Our plan was only to discover the secret, and now we have done that. I can think of nothing more we can do. Unless—unless we simply go to the Geets-kel and tell them what has happened and what we have learned and—"

Neric threw up his hands in exasperation. "Raamo. Sometimes I despair of your sanity, and of my own for choosing you as my accomplice. The Geets-kel are evil. Their motives are evil. We could do no worse than to tamely deliver ourselves into their hands."

"Evil?" Raamo said. "But why?" Bowing his head he pressed the palms of his hands against his forehead as if it were possible to catch and hold his thoughts and thus to still the turmoil of his mind. Long moments passed in silence. At last Raamo raised his head and looked at Genaa. She had not spoken for a long time. She was sitting very still, her chin lifted and her eyes glowing darkly.

"Genaa," Raamo said. "What do you think? What do you think we should do?"

"What you should do, Raamo, I cannot say. But I know what I will do and what I will never do. I will never take part in any plan to free the Pash-shan. And if I thought that it was possible for you and Neric to free them I would—I would go to the Geets-kel and tell them what you planned to do."

"I told you," Neric said bitterly. "I warned you, Raamo, about your precious Genaa, and you would not listen."

"It is because of your father, isn't it?" Raamo said. "But do you still believe that he was killed by the Pash-shan?

Even now that we know the Pash-shan are not sharp-fanged monsters? How could the Erdlings have killed him and for what purpose?"

"I don't know that," Genaa said. "But I know that my father went down to the forest floor to try to make contact with the Pash-shan, and he never returned."

"Aha!" Neric said suddenly. "Did anyone else know of his plans? Had he, perhaps, confided in a sympathetic Ol-zhaan? Did he seek counsel concerning his plan to contact the Pash-shan? If he did, he was probably taken not by the Pash-shan but by the Geets-kel. And that would explain many of the other disappearances of adult Kindar that have occurred in recent years."

"I thought of that," Genaa said. "I thought of the possibility that the Geets-kel might have somehow arranged for his disappearance. But they did not know. Before he left, he told me that *no* one else knew. He said he was only telling me so I would know what had happened if anything went wrong. He said he had been working on a theory concerning the Pash-shan, and that if his guesses were correct, he would be in no danger; but that if he did not return by nightfall, I would know that he would never return again, and that I should not wait and hope as it would only make the sorrow harder to bear.

"And then he left. I saw him go. I followed him until he began to climb down below the lowest branches. He never came back. I don't know what the monsters in human form who call themselves Erdlings did to him, but I know that he is dead. If he were not dead, he would find some way to let me know. So the Erdlings must have killed him. And so you see that I could never help you to free them."

Genaa had been staring down at the floor as she spoke, but now she raised her head and looked toward Raamo with eyes that were like dead moons. "I would help you, Raamo, if you were planning to kill them," she said. "My cause is still to rid Green-sky of the curse of the Pash-shan."

CHAPTER SEVENTEEN

*T*here seemed to be nothing more to say. Nothing could be said that would alter either Neric's or Genaa's determination to oppose evil as they saw it. And as for Raamo, he could find no words at all to express the fear that gripped him, a fear that arose from no identifiable threat but only from a tormenting feeling of uncertainty—an unaccustomed and torturous uncertainty that seemed to be pulling him into small painful pieces.

Before they left the D'ok nid-place, Raamo went to Pomma's chamber to tell her that they were leaving and to warn her to speak to no one concerning Teera, or of any of the things she had heard discussed that day in the common room. Hearba and Valdo having been summoned and bid farewell, the three young Ol-zhaan took advantage of the lull in foot traffic brought about by the approaching hour of food-taking and made good their retreat to the open forest. They spoke little as they skirted the city and approached the Temple Grove through hidden sidepaths. But when they had safely reached Neric's hideaway in the Vine-screen near the Great Hall, Neric once more confronted Genaa.

"I must ask for some assurance," he said, "for one promise."

"And what promise is that?" Genaa asked.

"An exchange, a promise for a promise. We will promise to let you know what we plan to do, if you will promise not to go to the Geets-kel until then. That you will wait until you hear our plans before you decide to betray us to the Geets-kel."

"And how do I know that I can trust you to keep your part of the promise?" Genaa asked coldly.

"Surely you do not distrust Raamo?" Neric said.

Turning to Raamo, Genaa held out both her hands. "Tell me you will do nothing without including me," she said.

"In mind-touch?" Raamo asked.

"No!" she said, impatiently. "You know I cannot pense. But if you tell me with your eyes and palms as well as your voice, I will believe you."

So the promise was given, and a pledge made to meet again in the same place on the next free day. Then the three prepared to leave the hiding place for the branch-paths of the grove. Since it was not yet dark, Ol-zhaan and Kindar helpers were still abroad on the grove branch-paths. Neric peered out cautiously through the Vine leaves. After several minutes he motioned to Genaa.

"All right," he said, "there is no one coming—no, wait!" Grabbing her arm, he suddenly pulled her back behind the Vine screen. There was another long wait before he turned to whisper, "It was that paraso, D'ol Salaat. He appeared very suddenly near the hall entrance and then went by slowly, looking in this direction. I hope he didn't see you."

Genaa's shrug made it plain that she could not be concerned with the actions of such as D'ol Salaat. She stepped out through the growth of Vine, and in a few seconds was strolling casually along the branchpath. When she had disappeared, Neric turned to Raamo.

"Do you think she will keep her promise?" he asked.

"She will keep it," Raamo said. "But I don't know what else she will do."

Neric sighed. "If only we could find out more—discover new information that might influence her. If we could find out more about her father. I'm almost certain the Geets-kel had a hand in his disappearance. In the days between now and the next free-day, we must think long and hard about what we have learned today and what we should do about it. If we are alert and diligent, perhaps we will find a way to learn something of great importance. But one last word of warning, Raamo. Be very careful when you are with D'ol Falla. There are rumors that she was once greatly gifted in the skills of the Spirit. I would remind you to guard carefully against revealing our secrets to her in your attempt to learn the ones of which she is the guardian."

In the days that followed, Raamo had much to occupy his mind. Most of all he thought of the Pash-shan—the Pash-shan who in horrible, half-seen forms had haunted his childhood nightmares, and who it now seemed were only other Kindar—Kindar who had been shut away, thrust down into darkness and transformed into fearful threatening legends.

He considered, too, what should be done about it, but he came to few decisions. There seemed so little that could be done. It could not be right and good that the Erdlings should be imprisoned and the Kindar deceived and deluded; but there was the Root, and no decision could alter the fact that the Root was indestructible. There were the rumors, of course, that the Root was withering. Teera, herself, was proof that somewhere it had withered enough to permit the passage of a small girl. Perhaps the withering would continue, and in the meantime there was the possibility that food could be supplied to the hungry Erdlings. But that would mean the Kindar must be told.

But should the Kindar be told? Raamo did not even know if Neric would agree that they should tell the Kindar, and he was quite sure that Genaa would not agree. And what would happen when the Kindar knew? When they saw that they had been deceived about the Pash-shan, would they then believe in nothing? And if they no longer believed in the Ol-zhaan, would they also lose their faith in everything and everyone? It seemed to Raamo that Kindar who had no faith in each other and in Spirit-life, would not be Kindar at all.

And what would happen when the disillusioned Kindar went to the forest floor and met their imprisoned kinspeople? What strange things, what thoughts and feelings, what habits and reactions would they learn from these mysterious, long-imprisoned Kindar of darkness?

Raamo pondered all these questions over and over again without arriving at any answers. But in spite of his unanswered questions and fearful uncertainties, he began to be aware that a belief was growing in his mind and becoming daily more strong and insistent. That belief was that knowledge of the true nature of the Pash-shan belonged to the Kindar, and that it could not be right to keep it from them.

During those days, Raamo also thought often of Neric's warning concerning D'ol Falla. Daily, as he made his way from the novice hall to the central platform and from there to the ornate door-arch of D'ol Falla's chambers, he reminded himself that he must be very careful. He must watch and listen for the slightest flaw in the mind-blocking of the old woman, at the same time being on constant guard to prevent any relaxation of his own. It was not an easy thing to do.

D'ol Falla was beginning to teach Raamo the many intricate rituals of the Vine, and there was much drill and repetition. But more than ever now, as he listened to the soft rasp of the old woman's voice, Raamo was tormented by the constant awareness of a dim uncertain questing, a blind searching that seemed to hover just beyond the edge of his own consciousness. And, more than ever, he found it hard to refrain from lowering his own barriers and reaching out in open response. But he did not. Instead he reminded himself of Neric's warning and firmly turned his thoughts to the ordered patterns of the ritual chants.

When the next free day finally arrived, Raamo hurriedly left the great hall after the morning ceremony, only to be detained by D'ol Salaat. D'ol Salaat, it seemed, had no plans for the free day and wanted to know how Raamo was planning to enjoy the hours of relaxation. It took some quick thinking and talking before D'ol Salaat could be sent on his way and Raamo was free to make his careful approach to the meeting place. Fearful that he would be keeping the others waiting, he finally pushed his way through the Vine-screen, only to find that there was no one there. Looking around, he noticed a large grundleaf attached to a Vine-tendril in such a way that it could not fail to attract attention. Someone had written on the leaf in large letters and left it where it was certain to be seen. Raamo had just begun to read the message when the Vine parted and Neric entered the hiding place.

"What is it?" he asked.

"A message," Raamo said, and together they read what Genaa had written.

"I arrived early and have gone on ahead, as I wish to speak privately with Teera. Join me there. Genaa."

"Privately," Neric said. "What is she up to now?"

Raamo shook his head. "I doubt that she will have much success," he said. "Unless she can somehow convince Teera of her goodwill."

"Goodwill!" Neric said. "When she has said that she would like to kill all the Pash-shan, even though they are only imprisoned Kindar?"

"I don't think she really meant it," Raamo said, "or, at least, she would not mean it if she took time to consider. But whatever her true feelings are—Teera will know. Although she cannot mind-speak, her pensing of emotion and feelings is very quick and accurate. She will know what lies beneath the questions Genaa asks her, perhaps better than Genaa herself."

"Perhaps," Neric said. "In any case, we had best hurry. I may not be noted for my skill at foretelling, but I feel quite certain that this private interview with the glorious D'ol Genaa bodes no good for our little Pash-shan, and perhaps no good for us."

Raamo and Neric made the long roundabout journey to the D'ok nid-place in a very short time, but it became obvious, the moment they entered, that the time had not been short enough. Pomma met them in the doorway, and her face was wet with tears.

"They've gone," she said. "D'ol Genaa came and

talked to Teera alone, and then they came out and went away. I asked them where they were going, but they didn't say anything except D'ol Genaa said to tell you that they were going to the forest floor."

"That was all?" Raamo asked. "She didn't say why?"

"No," Pomma said. "That was all she said. But I think she had been crying."

"Teera was crying?" Neric asked.

"No. D'ol Genaa."

"Genaa? Crying?" Neric said. He grabbed Raamo's shoulder. "Let us go quickly," he said. "There is no time to waste."

"What is it?" Pomma cried, bursting into a fresh flood of tears. "What is she going to do? What will she do to Teera?"

Quickly reassuring Pomma as best he could, Raamo joined Neric in the doorway to wait until a break in the traffic of strolling Kindar made it possible to hurry to the safety of their vantage point in the nearest leafy branch-end. There they paused long enough to plan their pursuit.

"She would have gone this way to the outskirts of the city," Neric said. "I would guess that if we go to the first uninhabited grund and seek out the first strong stand of Vine, we will not be far from the route taken by our impetuous colleague. She is in no mood for caution or patience, I think."

"Yes," Raamo said, "but she will not be able to move swiftly with Teera. If we hurry, perhaps we will be able to catch them before—"

Already pushing his way through the thicket of end-branches, Neric looked back to ask, "Before what? What do you think she plans to do with Teera? Do you think she plans to harm her?"

"I don't know," Raamo said. "It seems impossible. But if she forced Teera to tell her something concerning her father's death, and if in truth, the Erdlings were responsible—I don't know what she might do. She might—do almost anything."

"Aha," Neric exulted. "I am relieved, at least, that you are beginning to see more clearly. But do not berate yourself. You are not the first to be blinded by beauty."

Soon after crossing over from Grandgrund to the dense end-branches of the first forest grund, Raamo noticed a loosely twisted spiral of heavy Vine-stems passing directly through a leafy thicket of grundtwigs. Near the Vine, a grundleaf's succulent surface had recently been marred, as if by grasping fingers.

"This way," Raamo said, and swinging onto the Vine, he climbed quickly downward, with Neric following close behind. Within a very few minutes, they were standing, for the second time, on the forest floor.

As before, the light under the arching ferns was muted, deeply shadowed in shades of green, and in the still air the rich heavy scents seemed almost tangible to tongue and fingertips. No sound of voices or footsteps broke the silence, but here and there in the soft moss small rounded imprints were clearly visible. The imprints had quite possibly been made by the heels of small human feet, and led away from the Vine ladder in a southerly direction. Silently, alert for the slightest sound or motion in the surrounding undergrowth, Raamo and Neric crept forward.

In spurts and starts, losing the trail and finding it again, they zigzagged down long corridors under arching fern-fronds, and then crossed a more open area where the fern gave way to low, wide-leafed plants bearing enormous blood-red blossoms. Twice the trail led them across small crevices full of flowing water before it plunged back into a dense growth of·towering fern. Here the boles of the ferns grew so closely that the narrow pathway twisted and turned constantly and beneath the interwoven fronds the light faded to a greenish twilight. Bending low, peering, even feeling for the faint indentations, their progress had slowed almost to a crawl when a sudden sound brought them to their feet, staring at each other in wild conjecture. Far in the distance a voice, a thin childish voice, was shouting for help.

"Help," the sound came again. "Help me. It's Teera. Help me."

Frantically Neric and Raamo plunged forward, twisting and turning as they dodged around the fern boles and Vine-stems and scrambled over the decaying trunks of fallen rooftrees.

The call came again, much closer now, "It's Teera. Help me. It's Teera."

As the last shout died away, Raamo broke through a thick wall of undergrowth and stopped short. Following close behind, Neric was unable to stop in time to prevent a sharp collision. But the crashing of underbrush and the thud of colliding bodies went entirely unnoticed by the two people who were already occupying the clearing.

As Raamo scrambled to his feet, he saw that the two figures crouching in the center of the clearing were indeed Genaa and Teera. On their hands and knees, their heads hung low, the two girls might have been searching for something very small in the thick moss. Except that Teera was once again shouting, calling for help.

A cold wave of fear flowed up Raamo's spine, but he forced himself to move forward. He had approached to within a few feet of the kneeling Genaa when she turned suddenly and saw him. Her gasp of surprise turned into a shining smile as she leaped to her feet and threw her arms around him.

"Oh Raamo," she cried. "He's alive. My father is alive."

CHAPTER EIGHTEEN

*A*t Genaa's joyous cry, Teera finally became aware of Raamo's presence and turned away from the ventilation tunnel down which she had been calling. Getting quickly to her feet, she approached Raamo shyly, but with a smile almost as radiant as Genaa's own.

"Greetings, D'ol Raamo," she said softly, "and D'ol Neric," she added as Neric, whose progress had been temporarily impeded by a shortness of breath brought on by running at full speed into a suddenly stationary Raamo, finally staggered up.

"Greetings, Teera," Raamo said. "We heard you calling for help and came as quickly as we could. Were you in danger?"

Teera looked surprised. "No," she said. "I was just calling—" she motioned to the dark hole bordered by Wissenroot, "—I was just calling to the Erdlings to come and help us. But no one has come yet."

Genaa laughed, and there was a lightness to her laughter that Raamo had not heard before. "Let me tell you," she said. "Let me tell you what happened." Glancing at the still gasping Neric, a touch of her old mockery glinted in her eyes as she said, "You seem breathless, D'ol Neric. Please be seated. I have much to tell."

When they were seated on the soft turf of the clearing, Genaa began her narrative. "I decided to go early to the D'ok nid-place because I wished to question Teera concerning the disappearance of adult Kindar who ventured down to the forest floor—what was done to them and how they were disposed of. I knew such questions would frighten Teera and you would object if you were present." Genaa smiled ruefully. "The questions did, indeed, frighten her. So much so that I was unable to get a word from her, no matter how I threatened and pleaded. But then I became so troubled that I began to cry, myself, and I began to talk to Teera about my father. I don't know why. I have not been able to speak of him much to anyone since his—since he disappeared. But somehow I found myself crying and talking about him—how good and wise he was and how I had worshiped him—and, suddenly I realized that Teera had stopped crying and was listening very carefully with a strange expression on her face. I don't even remember saying my father's name but I must have in my raving, because when I finally quieted, Teera said, "I know a man named Hiro D'anhk. He is a teacher and a Verban.'

" 'A Verban'? I asked, and Teera explained that nearly everyone in Erda is either an Erdling or a Fallen—who are almost like Erdlings because they have been below the Root since they were infants. But there are a few who are not Erdlings or Fallen, and they are called Verban. The Verban are those who have been *sent* below the Root by the Ol-zhaan." Turning to Teera, Genaa asked, "Isn't that right, Teera? Isn't that what you said about the Verban?"

Teera nodded. "And everyone feels sorry for the Verban," she said, "because they have lost their people and all the things they were born to, like trees and sky."

"When I asked her how long the Verban named Hiro D'anhk had been in Erda, she said a long, long time," Genaa said. "It has been only two years, but that must be a very long time to someone like Teera who is only eight years old. When she described him, the Hiro D'anhk who is now teaching in the Erdling academy, I knew that it was he. So I asked Teera to come with me to the forest floor to help me look for a tunnel opening. And here we are."

"You were not afraid to come with D'ol Genaa?" Raamo asked Teera.

Teera shook her head. "Not when she wasn't angry anymore. I was afraid at first on the Vine, but D'ol Genaa told me to shut my eyes and climb by feeling, and when I couldn't see how far it was, I wasn't afraid anymore and I climbed like a sima. Didn't I, D'ol Genaa?"

"You did, truly," Genaa said. She laughed again. "Oh Raamo, I have never been so—"

"Great Sorrow!" Neric shouted suddenly. "Do you realize what this means?"

"Means?" Raamo said, and it was not until that moment that he began to think about meanings and significances, having been too much caught up in Genaa's Joy to think of anything else.

"It means," Neric said, "that there are still some among the Vine-priests who are capable of causing changes in the Root. *And* that new prisoners are still being added to those already below. It means that the mysterious disappearances of adult Kindar are no longer a mystery, and that many who were thought to have died at the hands of the Pash-shan are probably still living among the Erdlings."

"But if the Vine-priests can still influence the growth of the Root, why are they unable to control the withering?" Raamo asked. "Surely, if the priests could cause the Root to shrink enough to allow the passage of a full-grown man, and then regrow, they could keep it from withering."

"But there must be withering," Neric said. "Teera is proof of that, and I, myself, heard D'ol Falla speak for the choosing of Raamo *because* of the withering. With my own ears I heard her say that she advised Raamo's choosing, in spite of the dangers, because of the chance that his Spirit-force could be used to heal the Root."

"There must be an explanation," Genaa said. "If the Root can open enough to swallow my father, it can open enough to release him, and I intend to find out how it can be done." The soft shining was gone from Genaa's face and voice as she spoke, replaced by the old rigidity.

"It must be D'ol Falla," Raamo said. "If anyone can still change the Root, it would be she."

"You are right," Neric said. "It would seem that our answer lies with—"

"Look!" Genaa gasped, pointing toward the mouth of the tunnel. But when they all crowded around the dark root-bordered crevice, there was nothing to be seen.

"But I know I saw something," Genaa whispered. "From where I was sitting, I could see the mouth of the tunnel and suddenly there was a light and movement. I know I saw something move."

"Greetings, Erdling," Neric called. "We come in peace. Come forward and speak to us."

"Shh," Teera said, shaking Neric's arm. "You will scare him away. He can see you are an Ol-zhaan." Leaning over the opening, Teera called softly in her singing soft-voweled Erdling manner, "Please come back. It's Teera. It's only Teera Eld and some good Ol-zhaan. They won't hurt you, I promise. Please come back. We need you to help us."

As Teera's soft voice coaxed, a dim light began to be visible in the darkness of the tunnel. The light grew stronger, and it became evident that it came from a lantern. A hand held the lantern, a smudged and dirty but entirely human hand. It came closer and, at last, a face appeared out of the shadows. It was the face of a young man, whose eyes were large and white-rimmed, as if with fear.

"I know you," Teera said. "Greetings, Tocar. Don't you know who I am?"

"You—you are Teera, the daughter of Kanna and Herd, who will be gladdened to hear that you are yet alive. Your father still searches the farthest tunnels for you daily, although the date has already been set for your Ceremony of Weeping. How is it that—" The husky shaky voice with the strange intonations broke off sharply as Neric once again moved into the Erdling's range of vision. He was, once more, retreating down the tunnel when Teera called.

"Come back, Tocar. They won't hurt you. Come back, and I will prove it." Turning to Raamo she motioned for him to come forward, and taking his arm, she pulled at it until he knelt beside the tunnel mouth. "Put your hand down to him, D'ol Raamo," she pleaded. "Let him feel how you will not hurt him. Please, or he won't believe me and he'll run away and not help us."

Raamo's heart was pounding and a strange quivering in the backs of his legs was beginning to trouble him, although he did not know why. He knew now, beyond doubting, that the dim figure below the Root was Erdling and human, but something in the deep folds of his memory still whispered "Pash-shan." He leaned forward, extending both hands, and suddenly he was face to face with the Erdling, their eyes met and then their palms; and Raamo found himself pensing fear, and the recognition of his own fear, and then slowly a kind of bewildered but joyful relief. White teeth gleamed in the dim light as the Erdling's lips moved in a shaky smile.

"Greetings," the Erdling said. "What manner of Ol-zhaan are you that you wish no harm to Erdlings?"

"My name is Raamo, and I am one of many who would wish no harm to you if they but knew, as I do now, that the Pash—Erdlings wish no harm to Kindar. We have been wrong to fear each other."

"I am happy—in fact delighted to hear it," Tocar, the Erdling, said. He was grinning now, chattering nervously in his relief. "I can't say how delighted. I have never had such a fright as just now when I saw your white robes and realized that I was standing within a few feet of Ol-zhaan."

Pressing forward, Genaa interrupted. "Greetings, Tocar, I am Genaa. I would ask you a question of great importance. Do you know a man named Hiro D'anhk? He is an instructor at the academy of Erda—and a Verban. Do you know him?"

"Hiro D'anhk?" Tocar said. "Yes, I know him, or of him, at least. He is much respected in Erda as a wise and learned man."

"Could you go to him," Genaa asked breathlessly,

"and tell him that his daughter Genaa is waiting for him here, at this tunnel mouth? Could you show him the way?"

Tocar stared up into Genaa's radiant face, and for a moment he seemed to have been stricken speechless. But at last he responded. "Yes, yes," he said. "I can do that. It is a long way. Will you wait here?"

"I will wait," Genaa said.

"And the Elds? The parents of Teera. Shall I bring them also? They live farther away, and it would take somewhat longer."

"No," Genaa said. "Send a messenger to them with the news that their daughter is alive and well. But don't bring them here. We have not yet found a way to reunite her with them, but we will. You can tell them that."

"Yes," Teera said. "Tell them that the good Ol-zhaan are taking care of me, and that I get lots of food to eat. Tell them I will see them soon."

When Tocar had disappeared back into the dark depths of the earth, the wait began. As they waited, Neric and Raamo discussed the possibilities that had been opened by the discovery that Genaa's father was alive and below the Root. Obviously there was a way to pass through the barrier—but how, or where? Either the Root could be made to shrink, to shrivel or to draw back until the passage of a full-grown man was possible, and then to renew itself. Or else there was, somewhere, a hidden passageway through the grillwork of Root. A passageway, the location of which was unknown except to the Geetskel.

It was Raamo who suggested the second possibility. "It seems unlikely there could be such a place without the Erdlings having discovered it," he said. "But I have heard enough in D'ol Falla's classroom to make me think it is also very unlikely that the Root could ever have been made to alter its shape quickly. Even in the days of D'ol Wissen, himself, it seems that the spreading of the Root was very slow."

"Perhaps," Neric said. "But if such a place exists, how is it that the exiled Kindar, the Verban, do not return to it, and by it return to Green-sky?"

"Yes," Genaa said. "And how was my father made to pass through such an entrance. He would not have gone of his own free will."

"Then—" Raamo said, and stopped appalled at his own thoughts.

"Yes," Neric said. "Then the Geets-kel must have used—violence."

Although he had learned, in D'ol Regle's class, to use such offensive terms with historical calm, Raamo felt the color flooding into his face. That such a thing could have happened was unthinkable. That a Geets-kel, who was, after all, also a holy Ol-zhaan, could have—what? Raamo tried to imagine it. He pictured a group of Ol-zhaan—and a struggling victim. Would their hands be bare or would they contain some tool of violence, such as were used in the days before the flight? Did the Geets-kel possess and use such things? An image arose in Raamo's mind, an image of revolting obscenity: a human being, looking into the face of another, meeting his eyes, and sending forth pain or even death. In horror, Raamo struggled to close the eyes of his mind against the image.

"Teera." Raamo's horrifying vision was cut short by Genaa's sudden call to Teera, who had wandered to the other side of the clearing. The child returned running and skipping. Taking her hands, Genaa pulled her down to sit with them. "Teera," she said. "Tell us about the place where you came through the Root. Are you sure it was too small for a man to pass through?"

"I'm sure," Teera said. "It was almost too small for me. It was very tight, and the cold of the Root hurt me, and for a while I thought I was caught there and would never get free. But then the rain started and the wetness made me more slippery and I squeezed through. I had to get through because Haba was outside, in the forest, and I had to find him."

"And the opening, where was it?" Genaa asked. "How is it that others have not found it, and perhaps other small children squeezed through?"

"I don't know where it is," Teera said. "It was a long way down an old mining tunnel that no one uses any-more—there are lots and lots of them all over Erda—and then up a partly caved-in ventilation tunnel that went up to the Root. I was hiding when I found it, but I was lost, too. I'd been lost in the old tunnels for a long time when I found it."

"But you are sure that no one larger than yourself could get through it?"

Teera nodded firmly, and Genaa sighed, shaking her head. "I had thought that it might be useful to look again for Teera's tunnel, but it seems it would not."

"It seems not," Neric agreed. "It probably would not even serve as a means of returning Teera to her family, since she has gained so much in size since coming to Green-sky."

Conversation had died away, and Neric and Raamo had begun to wander around the clearing with Teera, leaving Genaa to watch alone beside the mouth of the tunnel, when a sudden shout brought them running

back. They found Genaa, clinging to a pair of hands that
were thrust up through the narrow opening and peering
down into the darkness. She was laughing and crying and
calling, "Father, Father, Father."

CHAPTER NINETEEN

***D**rawing back to the edge* of the clearing, Neric
and Raamo waited, not wanting to intrude on
the first great Joy of greeting between Genaa
and her father. After what seemed a very long time, she
turned and beckoned them forward.

As they approached, Genaa said, "This is my father,
Hiro D'anhk, and these are my two friends, Father, of
whom we have been speaking."

Below the tunnel opening a thin, dark-eyed face
looked up at them. The face was larger and more angular,
but possessed of the same brilliant beauty as Genaa's.

"Greetings, Neric and Raamo," he said. "My daughter
has been telling me amazing things concerning you both,
and of the great goal you have set yourselves." Stretching
his arms through the opening, Hiro D'anhk offered his
palms in greeting, but he did not, Raamo noticed, recite
the words of the Palm Song, nor did he use the respectful
title D'ol.

"I rejoice more than I can say," Hiro D'anhk went on,
"to find there are some among the Ol-zhaan who are truly
concerned with the welfare of the Kindar—of all the Kin-

dar, both above the Root and below. And I am even more joyful to find that my daughter is part of such a company. I could not wish her a better task in life."

"I have told my father of what we have learned," Genaa said, "and he desires to tell you his story. He says there is much in it that we should know."

Hiro D'anhk, it seems had, in the course of his studies at the Academy, become interested in the inconsistencies among the facts given about the Pash-shan. Unable to satisfy his curiosity, he had at last appealed to the Council of the Academy, a group of Ol-zhaan who were in charge of management of the institution, and asked for their permission to conduct a new and thorough study of the age-old curse of Green-sky, the dreaded Pash-shan. The Council had listened politely and a few days later had called him back before them to tell him that his request was denied. Firmly and emphatically denied, without reason or explanation. Being a noted scholar, whose studies had greatly increased the production of silk and helped to develop an efficient new system of sanitation in the cities of Green-sky, Hiro was not accustomed to such treatment. It was then that he had decided to continue with his studies on his own and secretly. Before long, however, he began to suspect that his secret was known, or at least suspected. Several times he was called before the Council and examined concerning the course of studies he was pursuing and the methods he was employing. This troubled him, since he had never before been subjected to such an inquisition. And then the blow fell. He was suddenly removed from his position as Director of the Academy of Orbora and transferred to the small city of Farvald, as a seventh-term teacher in the local Garden.

In Farvald he had, of course, continued with his studies, as well as he was able. One line of investigation that had proven most fruitful was his attempt to interview the friends and associates of all adult Kindar who had been lost to the Pash-shan in recent years. In these interviews a pattern began to emerge. Nearly all of the Kindar who had disappeared could be classified in one of two groups. Either they had been thinkers and seekers, people whose curiosity might have led them into danger, or they were orchard workers, whose daily labor brought them into closer contact with the Pash-shan than was the case with most Kindar.

In questioning the associates of the lost orchard workers, another pattern grew. Several, it seemed had, shortly before their disappearance, witnessed something concerning the Pash-shan that they had found most disturbing. Most had not disclosed exactly what it was they had witnessed, but a few had mentioned their determination to seek counsel concerning the matter—to go to the Ol-zhaan. Most significant of all, one orchard worker, before his disappearance, had told a fellow worker that he had *spoken* with a Pash-shan. Several years had passed since his disappearance, but the co-worker remembered it well. He had discounted the story, of course, he had assured Hiro D'anhk. Obviously the poor man had indulged in too many Berries, or, perhaps, neglected to wear his head shade in the open orchard and been stricken with sun-fever. But such a wild story was not one that was easily forgotten. Spoken with a Pash-shan, indeed!

Gradually an almost unbelievable but strangely seductive theory had begun to grow in Hiro's mind. He had begun to believe that there was a deadly secret concerning the Pash-shan, any knowledge of which was enough to doom a Kindar to oblivion. It also seemed to be true that the victim's disappearance occurred soon after the Ol-zhaan became aware of the individual's knowledge of the secret.

It was then that Hiro had decided to go, himself, to the forest floor in search of further information. On the day of his expedition, Genaa had witnessed his departure and had begged him to tell her where he was going. Thinking, as he did by then, that the Pash-shan were probably more pitiable than fearful, he had told Genaa where he was going and that he did not believe he would be in great danger.

He had not been long on the forest floor, however, when he heard the sound of footsteps behind him and someone called his name. He turned to see, not a Pash-shan, but the Ol-zhaan D'ol Wassou.

"I was apprehensive, of course," Hiro said, "but D'ol Wassou is an old man and quite frail, and I could not see how he could offer any immediate danger. His approach was friendly, even enthusiastic, as if he were relieved to see me. He spoke of how he had been sent with a small party of Ol-zhaan to search the forest floor around Far-vald for signs of withering of the Root and had become separated from the others. He wondered if I had seen them. He did not question my presence on the forest floor or express the slightest degree of disapproval. If I had been thinking clearly, I would have been warned by that fact alone, and it also should have occurred to me that our meeting—in all the vast and trackless stretches of the forest floor—could not easily be explained as coincidence. But I was not warned, and when he asked me to sit with him while he rested and refreshed himself from his food pouch, I agreed. Sitting together on the moss-covered remains of a fallen tree, we rested, and I accepted a drink of pan-liquor from his drinking gourd. I remember nothing more until I began dimly to return to awareness and found myself groping my way down an endless dark tunnel. I will never forget how slowly and painfully, and with what nameless terror, I began to realize that I was below the Root."

Raamo, Neric and Genaa had listened with fascination, and now Neric burst out in a frenzy of impatience. "But how? How were they able to open the Root for your passage?"

"I don't know," Hiro said. "The Erdlings believe that the Ol-zhaan can cause the Root to shrink away in an instant and return again, but I, myself, am not sure."

"Raamo has begun the studies of a Vine-priest," Genaa said, "and he thinks as you do—that changes in the Vine come very slowly."

"If at all," Raamo said. "I think that the Ol-zhaan may no longer be able to cause any changes."

"Then there is an opening," Neric said. "A permanent passageway."

"I have looked for one," Hiro said. "I have searched everywhere, and in particular in the area in which I was found wandering. But the potion I was given apparently allowed my body to return to life while my mind still slept. I had been wandering, perhaps for miles, before I returned to consciousness. And even after that, I stumbled on and on for an endless time through complete darkness before I was found and rescued by the Erdlings. It was impossible to guess where my wandering had begun. And my experience is not unlike that of every other Verban to whom I have spoken. All of them, *all*, had gone to seek counsel from an Ol-zhaan, or had been called before them, and all had been offered a friendly sharing of something that seemed to be ordinary pan-liquor."

Suddenly Neric sprang to his feet. "Enough," he cried. "We have heard enough. We know now what it is that we are facing. We know the full extent of the evil. Now all that is left for us to do is to move against it. We must begin to plan how we shall overcome the Geets-kel. It seems to me that our best course would be to call the people of Orbora together in the largest assembly hall and tell them everything. And then lead them to Temple Grove, where, with the strength of a thousand Kindar behind us, we will confront the Geets-kel."

Raamo found himself shaking his head. He felt strongly that the Kindar must be told, but the imaging that came to him as Neric described the telling was one of confusion and bewilderment—panic and desperation.

Genaa, too, seemed to find Neric's proposal somewhat impractical.

"Very grand and glorious, friend Neric," she said. "But it seems to me that the Kindar, after hearing our confusing and unbelievable story, might simply go home and curl up in their nids with bulging handfuls of Berries and think of less troubling things."

"Well, what would you do then?" Neric said. "What would you recommend?"

"I think our first concern should be to free the Erdlings," Genaa said. "Once they are free, the Geets-kel will have to listen to us. They will have no choice."

"But we don't know how," Neric protested. "It could take months, years even, to find the opening in the Root, and if in the meantime our search became known to the Geets-kel, as it undoubtedly would, we might well find ourselves below the Root—if not disposed of in some more complete and immediate fashion."

"And you must consider," Hiro D'anhk said, "what might happen if the Erdlings were freed suddenly among Kindar who were still ignorant of their existence and who would not know what to expect of them. If the Geets-kel were still not discredited in the eyes of the Kindar, who can say what evils might arise?"

"But what can we do then?" Neric cried. "What steps can be taken?"

"Small ones," Hiro said. "Small ones at first. Only evil comes from great changes made too swiftly."

"Raamo has not said what plan he favors," Genaa said. "Neric would turn to the Kindar and I to the Erdlings. In what direction would you go, Raamo?"

"I?" Raamo asked. "I feel the Kindar must be told, but I have not yet thought of how it should be done. I think that first we should—" He paused, and then found himself saying, "—I would go first to D'ol Falla. Yes, I would go to D'ol Falla."

There was a long tense silence as the others stared at him in amazement. But then the shocked surprise on Neric's face turned slowly to a blaze of controlled excitement.

"Yes," he said. "If we go quietly, the three of us—if we can go to her when she is alone in her chambers—we can make her tell us the secret of the passageway. And when that is ours, we will have a wedge—a lever of great power with which to pry the Geets-kel loose from their strongest vantage points."

"But what if she will not tell us?" Genaa asked.

"She is old and frail, and there will be three of us,"

Neric said, and it seemed to Raamo that his face altered strangely as he spoke.

Hiro D'anhk spoke from the shadow of the tunnel's mouth. "I don't know," he said. "I am afraid that the ancient D'ol Falla may have powers of which we are not aware."

"If she does, we will outthink her," Genaa said. "We will be careful to see that she does not summon help or make use of any tools of violence that she might have. We will come to her quietly as if to seek counsel, and then we will take hold of her, and we will not release her until she has told us the secret of the passageway."

"We will take hold of her—we will not release her." In Raamo's mind the words gave rise to images that mixed and swirled in patterns of meaningless horror. Patterns that intermittently gave way to another image—an image of youthful green eyes in an ancient face, and of something that searched blindly, pathetically, around the edges of his mind.

"I didn't mean—" he said.

But Neric had already gone, running across the clearing to retrieve Teera from where she still waited. And Genaa was bidding her father good-bye and setting a day for their next meeting.

The green light of the forest floor was deepening into blackness, and there was no more time for plans or explanations no matter how urgent. Teera must be delivered to the D'ok's nid-place, and Raamo and Genaa would soon be expected at the evening food-taking in the hall of novices.

By the time Teera was safely returned, the darkness was complete and the soft fine fall of the first rains had begun. Trying desperately to hurry, slipping on rainwet branches, groping for Vine and branch, the three young Ol-zhaan had no time for communion or conversation and little time for caution. And if there was one who followed close behind them, concealed by shadows and curtains of rainfall, they might not even have noticed.

CHAPTER TWENTY

When the three conspirators reached the Vineshrouded branchend near Temple Hall, they paused long enough for a brief whispered consultation.

"Shall it be tomorrow then?" Neric said.

"Tomorrow," Genaa agreed. "The longer we wait, the more risk we take that D'ol Falla will have heard rumors—and be prepared for our coming."

"But what shall we do—when we are with D'ol Falla?" Raamo asked.

"We will simply tell her what we know, and what we want of her," Genaa said. "And what we do then will depend on what she does. I am quite certain that the three of us, together, will be able to handle the situation, no matter what she chooses to do."

"And I agree," Neric said. "Shall we meet then on the central platform near the entrance to D'ol Falla's chambers at the seventh hour?"

And so it was decided. The three parted to return singly to their chambers and then to food-taking. Before too long, Raamo was swaying softly in the warm comfort

of his nid—and staring wide-eyed into the depths of a
dark moonless night. But his staring eyes saw much more
than empty darkness . . . Against the curtain of night,
images leaped and fluttered, flickered and faded. He saw
D'ol Falla. He saw the bird-bone frailness of her body and
the deeply probing gaze of her green eyes. He tried to
remember—to bring back in clear detail—the exact sensation that he had so often felt in her presence. A sensation of something watching, waiting—of a questing without words, a stealthy subtle sensing of his mind and
Spirit.

Was it evil, that questing? Was D'ol Falla evil? Could
she really, she the oldest and most honored of the Ol-
zhaan, as the leader of the Geets-kel have planned and
directed the disappearances of Hiro D'anhk and many
others? Would she, as Neric seemed to believe, arrange
for the disappearance of Raamo and Genaa and Neric if
she knew of their plans? And even more terrible to contemplate, did she have at her disposal tools of violence
such as were used in the days before the flight—instru-
ments of death that, at the touch of a finger, could take
the lives of those who opposed her? If she did possess
such things, would she use them against the three who
would stand before her in the morning, demanding that
she release to them the secret of the passage through the
Root? That such a thing might be possible seemed unthinkable. Yet Raamo knew that the bringing of death
had, in the days before the flight, been accepted and even
legislated by nations and governments.

At last Raamo slept, at first restlessly, dream haunted,
and then more deeply. When he awakened, it was as if
through a great distance of time and space. The rain was
over and dawn was not far away. But in the silence of the

predawn hush, Raamo awakened abruptly as if to a call. Startled, he lay stiffly, listening for a long moment before the summons came again, and he realized that he had not heard it with his ears.

"Come, Raamo." The voiceless call was distant and indistinct. "It is I, D'ol Falla, who summons you. Come now."

Without hesitation, Raamo rose from his nid, put on his shuba and, moving silently, left his chamber and the hall of novices. It was still quite dark and the leaves of the grunds still ran with recent rainfall when Raamo arrived outside the ornate doorway of the chambers of D'ol Falla. At the edge of the doorway, he stopped, staring. By the growing light, he could see that, although it was not yet dawn, the grill of tendril had been removed and the door hangings caught back by heavy cords—as if someone was expected.

It was that—the open doorway—that made him pause. The huge arch yawned darkly, expecting his arrival. D'ol Falla was awaiting him—or lying in wait. How did she know that he would come? And why had he come—so quickly without stopping to take thought?

Raamo had begun to move silently backward when suddenly D'ol Falla was standing in the doorway. Her green eyes glowed in the blurred beauty of her face like moonmoths in a misty night as she lifted her pale hands in greeting. "Ah, Raamo, you have come," she said. "Come in." And without protest or even hesitation, Raamo followed her into the great reception hall and through it to the mouth of a dimly lit hallway.

A dense predawn darkness obscured the magnificent chambers of the Vine priest, except where an occasional honey lantern marked the path they followed through hallways, rampways, and great echoing common rooms. As D'ol Falla led the way from lantern to lantern, Raamo followed, his feet moving slowly but steadily, while his mind seemed to be racing in frantic circles.

Why had he come? From whence came the compelling conviction that his coming, his response to D'ol Falla's summons, was inevitable—that he could not have avoided responding, and that even now, he could not turn and walk away?

At the end of a long narrow rampway, D'ol Falla stopped at what appeared to be a solid wall of frond-woven tendril. Removing a honey lantern from a nearby wall hook, she handed it to Raamo, indicating that he should hold it close to the tendril grillwork. By the light of the lantern, she quickly removed some cleverly concealed pins, releasing a panel that she then slid to one side. A small doorway was revealed and, taking the lantern from Raamo's hand, D'ol Falla led the way down a corridor so narrow that the wing-panels of his shuba brushed the walls on either side. This tiny corridor ended before what appeared to be an impenetrable barrier—the trunk of an enormous grund. Handing the lantern back to Raamo, D'ol Falla took from her waist-pouch a small piece of dark metal and inserted it into what appeared to be an intricate metal amulet that had been embedded in the trunk of the grund. She turned the metal to one side; there was a grating sound; and a door panel of solid wood swung open. D'ol Falla and Raamo entered a large room that had obviously been formed by hollowing out the interior of a grundtrunk. Hanging the lantern on a wall hook, she turned, and Raamo, who had been staring at his strange surroundings in amazement, found himself once again transfixed by the searching green gaze of her strange eyes. For a long moment no one spoke.

"What is this place?" Raamo said, at last. "Why are we here?"

"This is the Forgotten," D'ol Falla said. "It is here that the terrible memories of our tragic past are kept hidden away where they can do no harm. There was a legend long ago—long, long before the flight—that told of a box, a chest in which were imprisoned all the evils of the universe—until curiosity and disobedience set them free to torment humanity. This chamber is such a chest. Many great and dangerous evils are imprisoned within these walls."

D'ol Falla's gesture invited Raamo's inspection, and he once more turned his attention to his surroundings. Around the walls of the large room were many cupboards and shelves. Many of the shelves held books, or what appeared to be books, except they were much smaller and thinner than any Raamo had seen before.

"Are those books?" Raamo asked.

"Yes. On the wall before you and to your left, are many ancient books brought here at the time of the flight, and here—" she pointed to banks of shelves laden with books of a more familiar shape and size, "—here are histories of the early days of Green-sky. Diaries of the early Ol-zhaan chronicles of events and accounts of early studies and experiments. But much of the material included in these books is unknown, not only to the Kindar, but to most Ol-zhaan as well."

They moved on around the room, past the book-laden ranks of shelves, to cabinets of a different kind. These were wider and of greater depth, and they held many articles that were entirely unfamiliar to Raamo's eyes. Most of them were made, at least in part, from metal, but their purposes, the uses for which they were intended, were beyond his imagining. There was something, however, in their very shapes, in their blunt and graceless design, that spoke of brutal mindless energy materialized into solid form. It was as if the basest and most sordid instincts of humankind had, somehow, been embodied in matter and design. Raamo turned away, his mind recoiling in horror.

"These are weapons," D'ol Falla was saying. "Tools of violence such as were used by our ancestors in the days before the flight. This one, for instance, by only the slightest touch here upon this bar, is capable of destroying anything at which it is pointed, even at a distance of many yards."

Turning toward D'ol Falla, Raamo saw that she was holding one of the weapons in her frail old hands, her narrow fingers coiling tendril-like around its ugly surface. Roughly triangular in shape, the weapon tapered to a narrow orifice, a dark ugly mouth that seemed to reach out to Raamo as if in hunger. Raamo lifted his eyes quickly from the deadly mouth to D'ol Falla's face, seeking desperately to read there some reassurance, some clue to her intentions. But the bright green eyes looked back at him coolly from the withered face, and no shadow of thought or feeling answered his pensed entreaty.

"I have been informed," D'ol Falla was saying, "by those who keep watch for me, that you, Raamo, have been in contact with those who live below the Root, and therefore there are certain things that must be done quickly. But first there is a story that I would like to tell you. Let us sit here, by this table-board while I speak, for I am old and weary, and the tale will not be short."

Moving to a long table near the center of the room, D'ol Falla sank slowly into a chair, and Raamo seated himself at the other end. The old woman's eyes were still fixed on Raamo with unblinking intentness, and the cruel blunt shape of the ancient weapon was still heavy in her narrow hands.

"It is a long story," she began, "and a very old one. It is the story told by these books, and much of it is known to a very few among the community of Ol-zhaan, to those few who are known as the Geets-kel and to no one else. There are, I know, some parts of it that you have already learned. You have already learned, as have all Ol-zhaan, that our ancestors once lived on a large and beautiful planet, a rich and fertile world, blessed with every resource necessary to produce a complex and highly developed way of life. But, although they had managed, by their wisdom and knowledge, to find the means to banish most of the ills and evils that had plagued their early development, there was one great evil they were seemingly unable to control. And that evil was the curse of violence.

"In spite of their great wisdom and scientific skills, and in spite of the warnings of many of their Spirit-gifted leaders, they seemed to be unable to produce a society that functioned on any basis other than the pitting of human beings against each other in ways that inevitably produced pain and fear. Violence developed in ever more destructive and uncontrollable forms. This pattern continued for so long that there were many, even among their great thinkers and leaders, who felt that such things were inevitable, and that violence was so deeply ingrained in human nature that it could never be done away with. Yet there were, in the last days, some who felt that such was not the case, that all things were capable of change, and that there were many clues pointing the way toward new skills, new forces, even new states of being, which could produce a society free forever from the use of force. A small group of such men, scientists engaged in the study of developing human potentials, had created a laboratory, a school, where a large group of infants, orphaned by the latest in the endless series of wars, had been turned over to their care. The men had only begun their experiment, their training of the infants in the most advanced manifestations of the developing human Spirit, when the end came—and the flight began."

D'ol Falla paused, and for a moment her eyes closed and her head fell forward. She sighed deeply, and then, as if with great effort, she raised her head and once again the green eyes met Raamo's.

"The early days of Green-sky were a time of great change, of incredible adventure and exploration in the realm of the human Spirit. The scientists, who of course were the first Ol-zhaan, chose as their leaders two greatly gifted men. The first was a Doctor Nesh-om, who had been a leading authority in the old world on what had been known as psychic research; he had been a pioneer in the training of young children to make use of and develop their naturally evolving powers of mind and Spirit. The other was a Doctor Wissen, whose field had been communication with lower forms of life, and in particular, the control and development of plant life by means of psychic force.

"These two greatly gifted men, although very different in personality and temperament, were united in their determination to work for one sacred goal: the establishment of a society that would be free from every form of violence.

"The first years in Green-sky were a time of great, almost unanticipated, success. Nurtured in institutions that encouraged close communication with their peers and teachers, taught to accept and encourage every instinct that nourished loving interdependence, allowed to express themselves freely in song and dance and to seek comfort in ritual and meditation, the children grew in Love and Peace—and with absolutely no knowledge of the evils that had destroyed their ancestors.

"But as the children reached adulthood, a disagreement arose, and there were soon two factions among the Ol-zhaan. One group, led by D'ol Nesh-om, thought that as the children matured they should be told the complete history of their race and the tragic truth concerning the fate of their ancestors. D'ol Wissen and his followers believed that it would be better to allow them to remain completely innocent of such evil knowledge. Such a solution meant, of course, that there would continue to be Ol-zhaan, a small group who would guard the key to the Forgotten and who would carry the burden of the knowledge of evil. The debate went on for many years. These shelves contain many of the writings of D'ol Nesh-om and D'ol Wissen on this matter, setting forth their opinions and beliefs."

D'ol Falla paused as she motioned toward the bookshelves beside the table-board, but Raamo noticed that although her left hand moved in a sweeping gesture, her right remained clasped around the ugly triangle of metal. The whispery voice resumed, and the narrative went on.

"The writings of D'ol Nesh-om reveal that in his old age he had become obsessed by a single idea. This obsession took the form of insisting that the Spirit itself was threatened by the division of the people of Green-sky into Ol-zhaan and Kindar. At last, D'ol Nesh-om and his followers took matters into their own hands and began, secretly, to instruct a small group of Kindar concerning the civilization of their ancestors and the evil days before the flight.

"But then many things happened swiftly. D'ol Nesh-om died suddenly, leaving his small group of followers without a leader; and in order to end the dissension and protect the innocence of the Kindar, D'ol Wissen was forced to take steps.

"Therefore, a group of five Ol-zhaan and fifteen Kindar became the first dwellers below the Root. In order to explain their disappearance, the remaining Kindar were told that a party that had been sent to explore the forest floor had been attacked by a terrible tribe of monsters. Thus it was that the Pash-shan came into being."

D'ol Falla paused again, and Raamo nodded. "I know," he said. "I know about the Pash-shan being really only Kindar. But how were they taken? How were they placed beneath the Root?"

"They were heavily drugged," D'ol Falla said. "Then they were carried down to one of the enormous caverns that had been found to exist beneath the forest floor. And it was then that D'ol Wissen, by invoking his great force for grunspreking, caused the Vine to be transformed. The Root spread and grew, becoming impenetrable and indestructible, and at the same time other changes occurred. Changes which even D'ol Wissen had not expected or foreseen. The simple blossom of the native Vine was suddenly transformed into a thing of strange and illusive beauty; and the fruit, a small sweet berry, was found to be capable of producing a relaxed and peaceful state of mind when eaten often and in large quantities."

"How could they have done it?" Raamo said. "How could they have shut them away to live all their lives in darkness?"

"It was not meant to be forever. It was D'ol Wissen's intention to keep them imprisoned only temporarily—until they could be made to see reason, or until the Kindar were more firmly established in their habits of peaceful communion. Indeed, he left a secret opening in the Root for the purpose of releasing the prisoners, in the event that the Root could not easily be restored to its natural state. But somehow the time never seemed right—barriers once established tend to grow stronger. And the Pash-shan began to grow and multiply beneath the Root. Eventually, others were added to their number. By means of the secret opening, others were placed beneath the Root—all those who seemed to be carriers of the seed of violence or dissension.

"Then, of course, with the secret of the Pash-shan to protect as well as the secrets of the Forgotten, it became even more imperative than ever that the Ol-zhaan be perpetuated. So it was that the choosing was established and the future strength of the Ol-zhaan, and the Geets-kel as well, was assured.

"And so life has gone on in Green-sky and, although the use of the Spirit-skills has gradually diminished, there has been no increase in violence, and the people, Kindar and Ol-zhaan alike, have continued to live in peaceful contentment, until—"

D'ol Falla was silent and her eyes, which had grown pale and distant, became once again cold green moons that held Raamo motionless with their strange radiance.

"Until now," she repeated slowly, "when it has all been endangered by my own folly."

"Through your folly?" Raamo whispered.

"Yes, mine. Because it was I who insisted that you should be chosen. Because of minor problems, problems no doubt easily solved by less dangerous means, I urged the choosing of one who was known to be gifted with unusual Spirit-force, although I knew the risk involved in such a choice. And now the worst has happened.

"The worst—" D'ol Falla's thin voice cracked and her pale fingers twined convulsively on the ugly surface of the weapon that still lay before her on the table-board. "I am old," she said, "and if I break my vow and take upon myself the curse of violence, I will not have long to suffer the pangs of remorse, or to contaminate others with my evil. And since I alone brought this threat to Green-sky, it must be mine alone to—"

The old woman's voice faded into silence as if it took all her strength, every ounce of her dwindling energy, to lift the ugly mass of contorted metal that lay before her. Raamo sat paralyzed as the blunt snout lifted and turned in his direction. But then, suddenly, it fell back to the table with a dull thud. Grasping her throat, D'ol Falla had fallen back in her chair gasping, her face convulsed as if she was in extreme pain. As Raamo sprang to his feet, she slid sideways from her chair and sank down, the silk of her shining shuba billowing around her.

CHAPTER TWENTY-ONE

When Raamo knelt above the still form of D'ol Falla, he saw no sign of life. He could detect not so much as a flutter of eyelids, nor even the slightest rise and fall of breath. If she were yet alive, it seemed that she would not be for long. To go out and return with a healer would take a long time—perhaps too long. Running to the heavy wooden door, Raamo pulled it open and returned quickly to the still figure on the chamber floor. Slipping his arms beneath her, he rose carefully to his feet. Scarcely burdened by the weight of her frail body, he had begun to move forward when a voice spoke suddenly only inches from his ear.

"You may put me down now, Raamo. I am quite all right."

Startled for a moment into complete immobility, Raamo at last came to his senses and hastened to place D'ol Falla on her own feet. She was smiling, the green eyes glowing like those of a mischievous child.

"You are not—you were—" Raamo stammered.

"I was feigning," D'ol Falla said. "It was an experiment. I was only testing you—and more than you. I was testing a theory."

"Testing? I don't understand."

"Don't you? Where is the weapon—the tool of violence with which I was threatening to take your life?"

"Where?" Raamo turned quickly to look at the table.

"Why, there. There on the table where you dropped it."

"Yes," D'ol Falla said, "although it could easily be in your own hands now. You could easily, and for very strong and compelling reasons, have taken it into your own hands, and you did not."

"I—I—it did not occur to me."

D'ol Falla laughed. Raamo had not heard her laugh before. Like her eyes, it was strangely youthful. "It did not occur to you!" She laughed again as if with great Joy.

"Come, Raamo," she said at last. "I can see that you are beginning to wonder if I have lost my senses or eaten too many Berries. Let us sit down again, and I will try to explain. It is time now for you to hear a different history—the history of D'ol Falla."

It was then, as D'ol Falla and Raamo seated themselves once more by the table-board, that behind the old woman's back two figures emerged silently from the open doorway. Just inside the door, Neric and Genaa paused, their faces tense and anxious. But then, as Neric started forward, Genaa grasped his arm, and at the same time signaled to Raamo to remain silent. By turning his eyes quickly back to D'ol Falla, Raamo indicated his understanding. Making a supreme effort not to let his relief and Joy at the sudden appearance of his two friends show on his face, he told himself that he should have known they would find him. They would have waited for him in the dooryard until he was overdue, and then the open grillwork and the trail of glowing lanterns would have been all that was necessary for such as Neric and Genaa.

Apparently unaware of the two who stood only a few feet behind her chair, D'ol Falla was still speaking.

"You must hear my story in order that you may understand what I have done and what I am about to do. I entered the community of the Ol-zhaan long long ago, at a time when the burden of their secret had not yet caused the Geets-kel to oppose the choosing of all who were blessed with gifts of the Spirit. I had, in those days, an unusual gift of Spirit-force. Other gifts of nature were mine also, gifts of mind and body that I had done nothing to earn; but being young and untempered by life, I allowed myself pride in my good fortune—pride and an ever-growing ambition. During my novitiate, I surpassed all others in my studies; and at a very early age I was made a priest of the Vine, and soon afterward I was invited to join the Geets-kel."

D'ol Falla paused, watching Raamo's face intently. "You are, I know, aware of the secret organization known as the Geets-kel." Raamo nodded, and she went on. "There were at that time, only twelve members of the Geets-kel. Of the fifteen Ol-zhaan who sat on the Council of Elders, all but three were also secretly members of the Geets-kel, so that they easily controlled all the judgments and decisions of the Council. Except for myself, all of the Geets-kel were Ol-zhaan of great rank and honor, and I was yet to reach the twentieth year of my life. I was highly flattered to be one of such company—and very much in awe of my fellow Geets-kel. And so when, after my initiation, I was told the secret of the Pash-shan, although horrified, I did not question the values or purposes that lay behind the secret. I did not question even when, not long afterward, I was asked to accompany a Procession of the Vine, which carried, on its draped altar, the drugged body of an orchard worker who had grown too curious about something he had seen in the orchard tunnels."

Raamo gasped, and his eyes flickered for a moment past D'ol Falla's head to where Genaa stood, her face a painful mask of controlled anguish.

"So that is how—" Raamo said.

"Yes, that is how the taken—and they were, indeed, taken, but by the Geets-kel rather than the Pash-shan—reached the forest floor. And from there they were carried far into the forest to an opening in the Root. As I have already mentioned and, as you may have guessed, there is a permanent opening, designed and ingeniously concealed by D'ol Wissen himself. Through this opening the victim was placed in one of the many deserted tunnels that stretch out in every direction from the inhabited areas of the lower regions. There, due to the nature of the drug, the victim returns to consciousness and body strength, but for many hours, perhaps days, suffers from a form of amnesia. By the time his mind regains the capacity for memory, he has wandered far from the place where he had been deposited. Eventually most of these exiles are probably found and adopted into the society of the Pash-shan, but—" D'ol Falla's eyes fell and her voice sank to a harsh whisper as she went on. "—it is possible, probable even, that some perish of thirst or hunger, or even of the terrible fear they must feel to find themselves buried, trapped in the dark tunnels inhabited by what they believe to be inhuman monsters.

"I knew these things for many years, and yet I did not question. Even when I became the highest among the Vine-priests, and as such led every procession that carried a new victim to the opening in the Root—even when it became my task to offer the friendly drink that held the drug—even then I did not question.

"But a few years ago, I began to find myself consumed by a strange restlessness of mind and Spirit. Long before I had lost, with only slight regret, every vestige of Spirit-force; but suddenly I found myself yearning desperately to once again feel myself a part of the force that moves in and through the Spirit-gifted. To feel again the Oneness with others—with all life—all things." As D'ol Falla spoke, her eyes seemed sunken into darkness; and Raamo felt that all around her the air had grown empty and hollow with her longing.

"I set myself to regain some of my old abilities, using every ritual and exercise known, but without the slightest success. So then, being unused to failure, I set myself a new task, that of discovering *why* I had failed. If I could not regain my Spirit-force, I would at least discover why the skills of the Spirit were waning in Green-sky. The fact that this loss of Spirit seemed responsible for many of the problems that had recently been increasing—the illness among the Kindar, the overuse of the Berry, and, of course, the withering of the Root—made my quest seem all the more urgent.

"I turned first to the old books and documents, the histories and diaries written by the early Ol-zhaan. As first priest of the Vine, I had been assigned these chambers adjacent to the grundtrunk that held the secrets of the Forgotten, so I was able to spend much time here among the old records. I spent many days and nights in careful reading and in thought and meditation. It was while I was studying the accounts that told of the great debate between D'ol Nesh-om and D'ol Wissen, that I became aware of a growing conviction. I had become convinced that D'ol Nesh-om's vision had been the true one; that when the first Pash-shan were shut away and the Root grew and spread, the growth of the Spirit was over in Green-sky and its decline was assured. Gradually, after long hours of meditation and much painful mind searching, I came to the conclusion that, whatever the cost in danger and turmoil, the Pash-shan must be freed from their bondage and the Kindar from their ignorance—and that the land of Green-sky must no longer be divided into incomplete parts: Pash-shan, Kindar, Ol-zhaan, and Geets-kel.

"I began, then, to question others among the Geets-kel, cautiously and without stating my true feelings, so that I would not be suspected too soon and thus, perhaps, hindered in any plan of action I might later decide upon. I discovered that, while several among the Geets-kel seemed to share my uneasiness concerning the virtue of our position, there were none who were ready to risk a change, none who saw that Nesh-om's dream could not be protected by methods that denied the truth of that dream. It was not that they were cruel and unfeeling as much as fearful and unimaginative. For many, years of power and glory, of being set apart, had left them blind and rigid.

"Despairing of help from my colleagues, I could not think where else to turn, and for a while I tried to forget my conviction and continue my life as before. But this I found impossible to do. I became more and more troubled in mind and body until I was almost unable to eat or sleep and my days and nights blended in a continual nightmare of guilt and shame. Lying in my nid at night, the sound of the rain became a chorus of voices chanting the words of Nesh-om's oath. Over and over the words rang in my ears, 'Let us now swear by our gratitude for this fair new land, that here, under this green and gentle sky, no man shall lift his hand to any other except to offer Love and Joy.' And I knew that I could never again pretend that the hand that gives fear and mind-pain is not a hand of violence, whether the giving be by such as this—" D'ol Falla touched the triangle of metal, "—or by a drugged cup.

"And then one night I dreamed—or I thought at first it was only a dream—that a voice spoke to me as I walked down a long hallway. I turned to see no one, nothing except the endless hallway that stretched back behind me into the far distant past. I seemed to know at once that the voice was that of D'ol Nesh-om and he spoke to me of one who would come as a Chosen. 'This one,' the voice of D'ol Nesh-om said, 'by his very existence, will vindicate my dream and break the bonds of fear and pride. You will know him by his gifts of Spirit, and by the two who will accompany him and who will give to his promise, motion and direction.'

"I awoke thinking only that I had dreamed strangely and with amazing clarity, but soon after I heard of the child Raamo—and I began to work for his choosing."

D'ol Falla sighed and then smiled, though her smile was weary. "But then, Raamo, when you were among us, I was not certain. Your gifts of Spirit seemed quite limited. I was unable to reach you. And I was not until recently aware of your two fellow conspirators. I am, however, quite aware of them now, and it would be more seemly of them to come forward and be greeted properly."

A bit sheepishly, Neric and Genaa came forward.

When they had sung the greeting, they joined Raamo at the table-board as D'ol Falla continued.

"I was still undecided when, late last night, a certain young Ol-zhaan, who often seeks to curry favor with his seniors by spying and tale bearing, came to me with a story of following you three to the forest floor and observing you in apparent communication with a Pash-shan."

"D'ol Salaat," Neric sent, and Raamo nodded.

"I saw then that I had been too cautious and that I must act quickly or it might be too late. My sending, summoning you to me in mind-touch, was involuntary, almost unconscious, for I had no reason to think that I could make you hear me. But a few minutes later, I felt quite certain that you had, and that you would respond.

"And then you came; and your friends, who are obviously the ones predicted by my vision, have followed you. So now I am certain that my dream was a true foretelling, and that you, Raamo, are truly the one foretold."

"I?" Raamo said. "But I am not—I don't see how I can be the one in your foretelling. I have done nothing. It was Neric who discovered the secret of the Geets-kel, and it was he and Genaa who made the plans. They will tell you that what I say is true." He turned to his two companions for confirmation and found that they were staring at him strangely; and their eyes, like D'ol Falla's, were full of hope.

Suddenly Raamo was frightened, more frightened even than he had been when the tool of violence had pointed at his heart. He pushed away from the table-board, his hands outstretched as if to ward off danger. "I am not a leader," he said. "I think I am not even a true Ol-zhaan. I am only a Kindar."

"Raamo," it was Genaa speaking, "you do not have to

be a leader. As D'ol Falla heard in her foretelling, you are a promise. You are a promise that the way of the Spirit can produce a new kind of humanity, with new and higher instincts. It is not you yourself, Raamo, but those instincts that we must follow."

"Yes," D'ol Falla said. "Instincts such as the one that tells you that you are still Kindar. Think of the evil that could have been prevented if we had all known, surely and deeply, that we were all Kindar—that we have all always been Kindar together, no more and no less."

Raamo nodded slowly, somewhat comforted. A promise. The words repeated themselves in his mind. The words were beautiful, like a call that beckoned enticingly from a far distance. A distance that seemed suddenly to be almost visible, dim and obscure, but alive with beautiful and mysterious shapes and figures. He let the eyes of his mind turn inward, toward that far distance.

But now Neric, whose entire face had been a jumble of excited energy since he had first entered the chamber, burst again into speech. "We thank you, D'ol Falla—we are indeed greatly thankful to you—and *for* you—" his words collided with each other in his excitement. "—I feel certain—I think it is inevitable now that we shall triumph—but would it not be wise now for us to speak of what it is that we will do, and where we will begin?"

D'ol Falla laughed. "You speak truly," she said.

"And typically," Genaa interrupted, smiling. "But before we plunge forward into the future, may I have one moment to offer D'ol Falla my own thankfulness for a private matter. May I thank you, D'ol Falla, for driving an evil shadow from my mind. For more than two years now this shadow has tormented me, filling my mind with dark imaginings against the Pash-shan, first, and then against the Geets-kel. But today I saw myself in your story, and I saw how easily I could have walked your path—and the shadow was lifted. For this I am more thankful than words can tell."

D'ol Falla touched her palm to Genaa's cheek in a gracious gesture of acceptance. And then, sighing a little, she turned to Neric.

"You are quite right, Neric," she said. "It is time now for planning and action. There are many things to consider, many goals to be accomplished, and many evils to be avoided."

"Do you think that what we are setting out to do is really possible?" Genaa asked. "All the weight of years and numbers is against us. Do you truly think we can succeed?"

"I think it is possible," D'ol Falla said. "There will be many problems. For many years most of the Ol-zhaan have been chosen not for their gifts of wisdom and Spirit but for their capacity for blind loyalty to power and pride. It is not likely that such as these will easily accept a change that would threaten their glory. And it is impossible to know how the Kindar and Erdlings will react to each other. We must move slowly and carefully and take every precaution. It will not be easy. But we have, here among us, gifts that will help us greatly, and we have the Kindar who, in spite of all, are still greatly blessed by the dream of D'ol Nesh-om. I truly think that we may be able to rekindle the light of that dream in all Green-sky."

"And you, Raamo, do you believe that we will succeed?" Genaa asked.

Genaa's voice came to Raamo as if from a great distance; and turning his mind to her question, he realized that he had been far away in thought lost in a deep dream that had come upon him suddenly and with great clarity, just as had the dream that foretold the healing of Pomma.

"What is it?" he asked. "What question did you ask me?" He smiled ruefully. "I'm afraid I was dreaming."

"Of what were you dreaming?" Genaa asked.

"Of a promise," Raamo said. "I dreamed of a promise that has always been, and always will be."

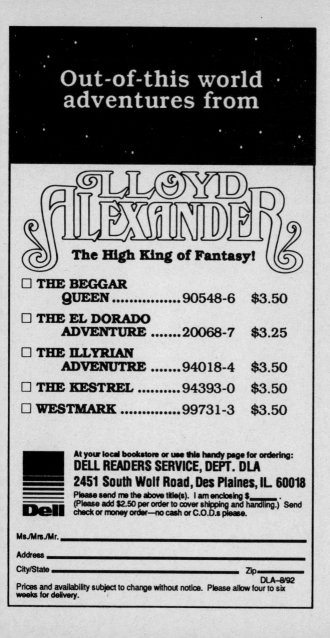